Mawgan

by Tony Dwelly

ISBN: 978-1-326-23218-4

Produced by simonthescribe

simonthescribe.co.uk

Contents

Mawgan
by Tony Dwelly

Chapter 1

In the late seventeen seventy's deep in the bottom end of Cornwall at a place called Prussia Cove, lived the Carter family probably the most famous smuggling family ever to reside in Cornwall.

But just along the coast was a man that history books seem to have forgot

His name Captain Mawgan.

Captain Mawgan ran a legitimate business he had four ships that took iron ore from Cornwall to South Wales and the North of Britten and brought coal back.

Like all Cornish sea men Capitan Mawgan could not resist a little smuggling, unlike the Carter family Captain Mawgan never sailed across the seas to smuggle he would buy his goods out to see from sea Captains who had travelled far and wide to shores many Cornishmen had never heard of.

Captain Mawgan was a kind man, and most of the local community benefitted from his smuggling escapades. He had everything a man could ever want. That is except the woman he wanted, a real beauty by the name of Tamasine Nancarrow, Tamasine was in love with the Captain, but would not let herself be involved with a man that was a womaniser, as the Captain had- had and did have many a women.

It was early afternoon Captain Mawgan was laying a sleep in a hammock in the garden of his cottage, his cottage was situated on the cliff overlooking a small harbour on one side and a secluded cove on the other, he lay there in just a pair of tight long johns and a vest tucked half in and half out. He was suddenly woken by a women's voice, "where are you Mawgan" the voice shouted.

"In the Garden who is it, I'm not descent mind". Came a rather startled reply.

"Don't worry it's only me and when are you ever descent". Came the reply from a soft voice with a little giggle in it that he then knew to be Tamasine.

"What have you come to lie down with me"? He asked as Tamasine entered the garden.

"Not a chance you know the deal you can have me when you give up all other women". She replied with that giggle still in her voice.

"I can't remember the last time I had a woman in my bed". Mawgan replied as he sat up and eyed her up and down.

"You might not have had anyone in your bed but I saw you coming out of Winnie Treewin's house this morning and it looked like you just got out of hers". The giggle had gone from Tamasine voice more now a sound of jealousy.

"What's a man supposed to do she didn't give me any choice, I said no because it's you I want, but she wouldn't take no for an answer". Mawgan smiled at her his eyes then shifted and peered down the front of her low cut dress.

Tamasine knew what she was doing as she folded her arms below her breasts making them rise even higher. "It's called will power and when you got that I'm yours". She said in a way that would have made any man drool.

"Are you sure you wouldn't like me to do something with those" Mawgan said as he looked further down inside her dress.

Tamasine looked up and down his tight long johns where something appeared to be stirring. "It's no good you hoisting your main sail the answer is no". She said knowing she was teasing him in a way only a woman like her could do. She put her hand on the hammock and pushed it like a swing.

"If it's not my body you want then for what do I have the pleasure"? Mawgan asked as he gently swung back and fro.

"Lily-Rose sent me to tell you there is a big storm brewing" Tamasine replied still gently pushing the hammock.

Lily-Rose was an old lady that had a small cottage down in the harbour she spent all her time sitting outside looking out to sea, her face had so many wrinkles I doubt there would be a man in the village that could count them, no one knows how old she is people in their seventy's say she has always looked the same Lily –rose always says birthdays. I have never had birthdays.

2

Every one took notice of what she said if Lily –Rose says there is going to be a storm. Then there is going to be a storm.

"You better let Lowenna know there will be boats sheltering in the bay tonight" Mawgan shouted as Tamasine gave one large push on the hammock and made her way towards the gate and left to tell Lowenna about the storm.

Lowenna was a large woman who ran the local tavern which had hot baths in the back; she had a few girls that would do a little more than wash your back for a copper or two.

Mawgan went and got dressed he then returned to the garden where he stood telescope in hand looking far out to sea; he could see a number ships out on the horizon he wondered how many would come in to the bay for shelter from the expected storm.

The wind had started to increase Mawgan was stretching up to let it hit him full on the face; he was then interrupted by Lowenna. "Afternoon Captain" she said as she entered the garden.

"Did you get the message about the storm"? He asked.

"That's why I'm here do you think there will be boats in for shelter".

"You can count on it, all good for business". Mawgan smiled at her. "Tell me what a man can expect for six pence at your place these days". Mawgan asked with a large grin on his face.

"Why don't you come down and see one night, I might give you six peneth worth for free." Lowenna said as she put her large arms around him and pulled him hard in to her big bosom.

"You never know I might take you up on that one day, but I'm still saving myself for Tamasine". He replied with a smile.

"She still teasing you then, she's a beauty by no mistake, but I know you Mawgan you've never gone hungry". Lowenna replied as she almost squeezed every breath out of him.

Mawgan pulled away from her clutches and picked up his telescope again and looked out to sea. "There's a vessel sailing this way I can't quite make out her flag though". He said.

3

"I better go and get the fires burning to heat the baths; I came up for some flagons of rum and French brandy". Lowenna said, her mind had now turned to making money.

"I'll send Willy down with some latter". Mawgan replied. "What do you want a couple of gallon of each".

"Four if you got um". Lowenna replied. "O" and don't forget my offer". Lowenna smiled and left the garden.

Willy was a bit of an odd job man, he kept pigs at the back of Mawgan's cottage and that's also where he slept. He would also sail a small sloth for the Captain out and fetch the contraband from the large ships that sailed bye. He was truly loyal to the Captain and would do anything for him after all the Captain saved his life about ten years before.

It had now started to rain Mawgan shouted loud for Willy to come, and within a couple of minutes he appeared, "have you got your cart" Mawgan asked.

"*E's* out on the cliff". Willy replied in his broad accent.

"Take these flagons down to Lowenna will you". Mawgan asked, as he passed him the flagons two at a time. Mawgan started to sniff loudly. "Man you are stinking" He caught hold of Willy's coat and pulled it up to his nose.

"*Tis* the pigs *Cap'n*" he replied.

"You better have a bath whilst your there". Mawgan replied taking two pence out of his pocket and passing it to him.

"I don't suppose *E* could run to four pence, could *E,* only they tell me you get a little extra for four pence". Willy said excitedly.

"What you get for four pence you can do yourself". Mawgan replied with a laugh.

"Well could *E* manage sixpence then"? Willy replied still looking excited.

Mawgan took sixpence out of his pocket". No drinks mind I might need you to night" he said as he tossed the coin to Willy.

"Thank *E Cap'n* I won't want no drink". He said as he excitedly ran and got his cart. Willy's cart had large wheels with extra long handles making it easier to push; Joseph the blacksmith had made it for him.

Mawgan returned to the garden and watched out to sea again the large vessel was now quite close to the shore. He could see a body of men dropping the sails and stowing them away, his eyes were drawn to the captain standing on the bridge, he too telescope in hand. Well I'm buggered Captain Louie from France sailing under the British flag he's taking a chance Mawgan whispered to himself.

With thunder and lightning all around them and rain pelting down Mawgan never took his eyes off the ship. He could see what looked like a man motionless at the stern of the ship, was it a man or a piece of wood he kept asking himself as it looked very dark.

Mawgan stood there for almost an hour watching wondering if anyone was coming ashore when almost like a mass exodus four boats where lowered over the side and men started to row towards the shore two boats looked like they were heading for Penzance but two were heading Mawgan's way with Captain Louie standing in the front of the first boat that was being tossed from side to side.

The image at the stern of the ship anchored out in the bay was still motionless is it a man was he dead, or just a large chunk of timber. Mawgan thought to himself as he closed in his telescope and made his way down to the little harbour.

He had just reached the harbour when the first boat arrived and Captain Louie jumped out. "Bonjour Cap-e-tan Mawgan". He shouted in a French accent as he landed on the quay.

"Bonjour yourself". Mawgan replied. "Why the English flag"? He asked as he embraced Louie like a long lost friend.

"I am English now like you". Louie replied with a big grin on his face.

"English I'm Cornish and abide by Cornish laws not English and I will always sail under the Cornish flag". Mawgan replied loud and proud.

"My dear Cap-e-tan you should sail under whoever is the best at the time. Now my ship he have thirty six guns and the French navy want to impound her and take her to America to fight you English. So Cap-e-tan

Louie very clever he sail out of Roscoff under English flag and sail to India and pick up cargo bound for England".

"If the English navy know it's you the will blow your ship to bits" Mawgan said with some note of concern.

"The Navy won't touch me I have a prisoner under orders of your King". Louie replied with a bit of a smirk.

"What prisoner is that then? He must be a proper criminal to bring him all this way".

"Ramjam the Indian". Louie replied. He was found in bed with the Earl of West Moorlands daughter. The Earl wants him so he can see him flogged and hung".

"Was the girl not willing?" Mawgan asked thinking it a bit harsh to hang a man for bedding a woman.

"In love with the man, she claimed as did he". Louie answered shaking his head in disconcerting way.

"Tell me what other cargo have you on board?" Mawgan asked wondering if there was a little business to be done.

"Nothing for you my friend I have silks and spices a special shipment paid for by the king of England. He put his trust in Cap-e-tan Louie and his crew.

"You've left all that on bored with no crew to guard it". Mawgan asked with some surprise.

"The canons are loaded and my five best marksmen are ready for action". Louie replied with an air of complacency.

"I don't expect there will be many sea rouges out to night". Mawgan laughed.

"Tell me my friend is the beautiful Lowenna still in business? I'm in such need of a great woman". Louie licked his lips in anticipation as he asked.

"She is up there". Mawgan replied pointing over to the pub on the quay side. It had smoke belching out of the chimney's from the large fires that where heating the water for the baths.

"Cap-e-tan Louie go now and have a large long soak with the lovely Lowenna". Louie leaned forward and kissed Mawgan on both cheeks.

6

As he left Mawgan wiped his cheeks in his sleeve. "Bloody French men". He said under his breath.

The rain still tipping down and the wind blowing at a rate of knots the sea was breaking up over the harbour wall.

Chapter 2

Mawgan had returned to his cottage where Willy was sitting outside in the rain. "You spent my sixpence wisely I hope". He asked in a jokily way.

"The lovely Lowenna bathed me *er* certainly knows *ow* to wash a man". Willy replied the smile on his face that said all that needed to be said.

Lowenna was rather a large women in every aspect, but a more cheerful women you would never find. She had put a smile on many a man's face.

"I must get to me bed now *Cap'n*".willy said. "If you have no more choirs for me".

"I do have a big choir for you were going on a mission". Mawgan replied full of enthusiasm.

"Where's *us* going *Cap'n"?* Willy asked knowing that a mission with Mawgan would be full of excitement?

"We are going to rescue an Indian". Mawgan replied.

"Is that wise, *Cap'n* Joe told me bout Indian's, *E* said they *ad* skin as red as the sunset over St Ives, feathers in their *air* like a Peacock on *eat*, axe's that would kill a man with one blow, and bows that would fire arrows straighter and further than a musket would fire a lump of lead". Willy had the look of fear on his face as his mind was in over drive.

Mawgan started to laugh. "Wrong Indian" .He chuckled.

"Is there more than one Indian?" Willy asked with a little surprise how could there be more than one Indian he thought.

"There sure is you have the Red Indian's in the Americas that's the Indian you are talking about. But there are people from India and that's who we are going to save.

"How far *us* going"? Willy asked full of excitement.

"Out to the French mans ship. Now I need you to fetch eight of our men, men that can row mind". Mawgan paused and with a bit of thought he said. "Perhaps five men. Tamasine and Winnie they can row as well as any man, and of course you, you can row as well as any of them. Of course that's if Lowenna has left you with any strength". Mawgan taped him on the shoulder and laughed as he said it.

"*Er* gave me strength *Cap'n* so much so I could row to America".

"Well we aren't going that far now go and tell them all to be down in the cove, at let me see". Mawgan paused for a second. "The storm should have abated at around midnight, give it an hour for the swell to drop, be down in the cove at one that will give us half an hour before the turn of the tide".

"I''I''*Cap'n* ". Willy replied as he turned and ran up across the cliff.

I wasn't long before Winnie had come down to Captain Mawgan's cottage; "You need me tonight". She asked as she stood in the cottage doorway.

Mawgan was in a tiny kitchen in just his long johns he was stopped over a large tin bucket dragging a cut throat raiser carefully over his face.

"I need you now". Mawgan replied in a soft voice.

Winnie walked over and gently took the razor out of his hand and put it down to one side, she picked up a towel and wiped the soap from his face, and she put the towel down and kissed him gently on the lips.

Mawgan lifted her up and sat her on the small table that the bucket was on, the bucket tittered on the edge, he started slowly to undo the lace that was down the front of her dress, as he pulled the lace out, each one exposed a little more of her breasts, Winnie was looking down at what he was doing and smiling neither of them uttering a word

Just as he undone the last one with her breasts fully exposed the cottage door opened Mawgan a voice shouted, a voice he knew to be Tamasine's.

Mawgan quickly pulled over a curtain that divided the kitchen from the rest of the cottage. Coming he shouted as the bucket went crashing from the table and spilling water over the floor.

"What was that"? Tamasine shouted rather startled. She went over and pulled the curtain back to see Winnie trying to quickly lace up her dress. "You bastard!!" she shouted as she turned and made her way to the door.

9

Mawgan was quickly out the door after her. "Wait". He Shouted. "It's not what you think".

"It's everything I think". Tamasine turned and faced Mawgan. "You promised me no more women". She sobbed. "I thought this time I could believe you. I came to you tonight; you could have had me tonight, but not now not ever". Tamasine turned and ran up the hill tears trickling down her face.

Mawgan returned to the cottage. "Forget her Winnie said as she put her arms around him".

"I can't why have women got to have things so complicated. I love that girl and I would give up everything I have for her". Mawgan said as he pushed Winnie away.

"Don't give me up". Winnie said with a smile?

"You don't need me you got more men friends than a ship got crew". Mawgan replied looking somewhat dejected.

"Saying things like that can give a girl a bad reputation if you aren't careful". Winnie replied as she was still lacing up the front of her dress teasing Mawgan as she did it.

"Don't worry about that you already have one". Mawgan replied as he put his arm around her and smiled.

"Tamasine is right you are a bastard". Winnie replied, with the most beautiful smile.

"I will not fall for your charms any more. From now on it stays in my pants. I will not let Tamasine slip away; I can't lose her forever". Mawgan was now talking quite serious.

"I think you should everyone knows you are meant for each other, and besides I wouldn't want you when your old with a beard down to your belly, like old Janna Prowse" . Winnie replied still fumbling around with the last bit of lace.

"Here let me". Mawgan replied as he caught hold of both ends of lace.

"That's a first you doing it up". Winnie whispered she wouldn't have minded either way.

"Any way what makes you think I will end up like Janna Prowse". Mawgan chukeled as he took his hands away from her dress and rested one on each of her shoulders.

"As I see it most men do, they don't wash, don't shave, dress in rags and smell of fish".Winnie looked up at Mawgan and kissed him on the cheek. "But I can't really see you like that". She said "Now shall I make you something to eat before are adventure; as Willy called it"?

"I think that's a wise move". Mawgan replied.

Tamasine had stormed down the cliff towards the quay she was just passing Lilly-Rose who was sitting outside of her cottage; Tamasine hadn't even noticed her sitting there in the pouring rain when she shouted out. You look troubled my dear.

Tamasine stopped and turned towards her. "Men!!" She said firmly as she walked over and sat down beside Lilly her hair dripping water and her cloths soaked through.

"Men is it or a Man?" Lilly replied quite calmly.

"A man you know who".

"I do indeed, an honest man a good man a man anyone would be proud to call a friend, a man you are deeply in love with".

"I know he is all those things and I don't want to share his love I want him to myself". Tamasine sighed. "Just now I walked in on him and that Winnie as if she hasn't got enough men; she should be in the tavern with Lowenna".

"My dear have you ever known Lilly to be wrong things will turn out right for you, might not quite be yet but trust me it will happen".

"You're just saying that to make me feel better". Tamasine said, wiping a tear from her eye.

"I wouldn't do that, I do know what will happen you will have many adventures along the way, and you will think it will never happen, but the man you love will be yours and yours alone".

"Then why won't he love me now I would have given myself to him tonight if she hadn't been there".

"Just think to yourself he will be mine one day. Think of all the good he does you won't find another parish any ware that a man has given so much; no child has gone without in our parish he has made sure of that".

"Yes he probably fathered them all". Tamasine replied quite abruptly.

"Now dear you go with him to-night he will need you, this is the first of your adventures together". Lilly-Rose looked at her and smiled her wrinkled face could tell a thousand tells.

Chapter 3

One AM down in the cove Mawgan and Winnie where waiting for the others Willy was next followed by the other five men.

"I don't think Tamasine is coming". Winnie said.

"Don't count on it". Came a voice from the rocks as Tamasine appeared.

"I wasn't sure you would come". Mawgan said looking rather pleased that she had turned up.

"Why not I said I would didn't I". Tamasine was going to play hard to get.

"I just thought with what happened earlier you might not forgive me". Mawgan said as he put his arm around her.

"O I haven't forgiven you, there is nothing to forgive you for, I know now that you would sooner be with her than me". Tamasine pointed to Winnie.

"You know that's not true, it's you I want". Mawgan was afraid he had blown it forever.

"I thought we were here to free the Indian". Winnie said trying to change the subject and get everyone moving.

"We are indeed". Mawgan said as he went over with the others and they all pushed the boat in to the sea.

They rowed hard and quick it was nearly low tide the idea being that the tide would turn when it was time to come back and the tide coming in would help them.

"Where's us going to *ide* the Indian". Willy asked.

"We will take him to the Mount, Eddy the harbour master will hide him until Louie has gone". Mawgan replied as he wiped the sweet from his brow.

They rowed hard until they got close to the ship. "Stop". Mawgan whispered. "We are making too much noise". He took off his shirt and tore it in to strips. "Wrap these around the rowlocks he whispered it will quieten the oars". He handed a strip to each of them.

The wrapped them around the rowlocks and started to row again this time much slower and gentle trying not to make any noise. They got close to the side of the boat where the Indian was tied. "*Ow's* us going to get up there". Willy whispered with a little concern.

"We will have to go gently around the ship until we find a ladder". Mawgan replied.

They made their way along the ship by pushing on the side of her they reached the other end of the ship were a rope ladder dangled.

Mawgan caught hold of the ladder. Make your way to the back he said, if you here any trouble just row like hell". He whispered as he climbed the ladder his heart pounding like Joseph the blacksmiths bellows.

Mawgan pulled the ladder up when he reached the top folding it up as he pulled it. When the ladder was completely up and he was on the deck he slung the rope ladder over his shoulder and started to creep to the rear of the ship. When he got level to the Indian he gently lowered the ladder down over the side to the others in the boat bellow. He was finding it hard to believe that they were having no resistance. He crept over and looked down into the galley below, he soon saw the reason why, there were empty rum bottles scattered on the floor and Louie's crack shots where all asleep on the floor. Mawgan crept over to the Indian who was tied to a mast his head was flopped forward and he made no movement, not even when Mawgan cut him loose he just collapsed in his arms, Mawgan quickly flung him over his shoulder and gently carried him down the ladder on to the boat below, he laid the Indian out in the bottom of the boat.

"Now row gently away and make for the Mount". He whispered his heart still racing.

"Is he dead"? Tamasine asked as they started to row away towards St. Michael's Mount first slow and gentle and then quickening the pace.

"No he has a strong heart beat I think he has been given something to knock him out". Mawgan left his ore go and placed his hand on the Indian's chest.

"*Ow's* us going to land *Cap'n tis* low tide". Willy asked taking one hand from the ore and rubbing his chin.

"We will have to land him on the west side". Mawgan replied.

They rowed round the back of the island and got in close to the rocks on the west side, Mawgan climbed up over the rocks, he soon made a hastily retreat. "What up *Cap'n*". Willy exclaimed.

"It's the Carters they are unloading gin there, we can't leave him here now".

"What's us going to do *Cap'n*". Willy was now sounding anxious and excited.

"He will have to come back with us. We will have to row hard as Captain Louie and his men will soon be returning to his ship". Mawgan pushed the boat away from the rocks and they all lowered their oars to the water.

"He can come and stay at my place". Winnie said as she looked up and down his body.

"I don't think that wise we all know what happens to men at your place". Tamasine replied with a note of sarcasm as she pulled hard on the oar.

"At least I know how to make a man happy". Winnie replied as she too pulled hard on an oar.

With the tide with them they were heading back at a fair rate of knots. "I think we should put Ramjam to stay with you Tamasine. If that would be all right". Mawgan asked as he knelt down beside Ramjam.

"That's fine". Tamasine replied thinking she had one over on Winnie.

"One thing for sure he will keep his trousers on staying with you". Winnie laughed but had the look of disappointment on her face.

Just as they reached the cove and dragged the boat up on to the beach Captain Louie and his men rounded the corner from the Quay, Mawgan and his team just managed to get out of site and make their way up to his cottage, he had Ramjam over his shoulder when they entered the cottage Mawgan flopped Ramjam on the bed. "You've put him in my place". Winnie said thinking this would upset Tamasine.

Tamasine was having none of it, she had a new plan tease and play hard to get.

"You should all go and get some sleep and thank you all for tonight, not a word to any one mind". Mawgan took a small hessian bag out of his pocket it was tied around the top with a piece of cord, he undone it and took out some coins he gave each of the rowers a shilling.

"I'll take mine in kind". Winnie said as she got as close to him as she could.

"You'll have a shilling or nothing". Mawgan replied as he put a shilling in her hand.

"Let's get Ramjam over to my place". Tamasine said as the others left.

Mawgan picked him up and put him over his shoulder and carried him up to Tamasine's. "Shall I lay him on your bed"? Mawgan asked.

"You will have too. I will sleep on the floor by the fire". Tamasine replied as she held the door open for Mawgan to get through.

"The first time I've seen your bedroom". Mawgan said as he smiled at her.

"Make the most of it it'll be the last". Tamasine snapped back she had made her mind up she would let him think she was any longer interested in him.

"I hope you say that in jest". Mawgan would never give up. "I will stay with you until he wakes". Mawgan said.

"That might not be till morning". Tamasine was at the pump in the kitchen.

"Then I will have spent the whole night with you". Mawgan replied as he sat on the bed beside Ramjam.

Tamasine had got a bowl of water and sat on the bed and gently bathed his forehead. "Look"!! She said as she pulled his sleeves up a little further and showed rope marks that had left his wrists raw.

"Look at his ankles". They are as bad Mawgan replied.

Mawgan stayed for almost an hour before he said he must go as Captain Louie might come looking for him. "Are you sure you will be all right when he wakes". He asked.

"I'm sure". Tamasine replied with a smile.

Mawgan went down to his cottage hiding behind a tree in his garden he could keep an eye on Louie's ship. He could see him on board waving his arms like someone completely out of control. It wasn't long before Louie was back in the rowing boat and making for Mawgan's bay. As he got close to the sure Mawgan quickly went in to his cottage and striped down to just his long johns, there was soon a large bang on the door. "What is it do you know what time it is". Mawgan shouted.

"It's me Cap-e-tan Louie". Came a rather loud reply.

"What do you want"? Mawgan replied as he opened the door pretending he had just got out of bed.

"It is the Indian I have lost the Indian, Cap-e tan Louie has lost the Indian".

"How do you mean you've lost him"? Mawgan replied trying to keep a straight face and a look of surprise.

"What Cap-e-tan Louie do say he has gone".

"Gone gone where!! You had your crack shots guarding him". Mawgan replied finding it difficult not to laugh.

"Drunk they are all blody drunk, they will be flogged to an inch of their death; it's no joke three hundred genies they pay me to bring Ramjam alive to Bristol".

"Is that wise to flog your men you might need them if you find you're Indian". Mawgan hated violence.

"You might be right I will send all my men in to Penzance and turn the place upside-down Cap-e-tan Louie will find the Indian".

"I don't think you should do that ether; just imagine what would happen if fifty French man went on the rampage in Penzance a lot of them would be killed".

"Cap-e-tan Mawgan always was so wise what does the Cap-e-tan suggest Louie do". Captain Louie looked bewildered.

"I suggest you sail on up to Bristol if I find your Indian I will bring him to you for fifty genies". Mawgan replied.

"Cap-e-tan Mawgan you are a true friend but thirty genies would be better".

"Forty genies then as we are friends". Mawgan held his hand out for Louie to shake.

Louie avoided his hand but leaned forward and kissed each of Mawgan's check's I hope to see you in Bristol he said as he turned and started to walk back to the bay.

"O how will I recognise this Indian"? Mawgan shouted.

Louie turned. "That's easy Cap-e-tan he shouted it will be like looking at a black bird in a seagull's nest".

Once Louie had left Mawgan quickly got dressed and made his way back up to Tamasine's. He arrived just as Ramjam was waking up he could here Tamasine saying. "Me Tamasine you safe now".

Mawgan went in to the bedroom were Ramjam had curled up in the corner of the bed with a complete look of fear on his face. "How is he?

"Scared stiff". Tamasine replied as she got up of the bed.

"My name is Mawgan and this is Tamasine we rescued you do you understand". Mawgan spoke in a drawn out way as if it would be hard for Ramjam to understand the language. "We are your friends". He continued.

Ramjam noded.

"We" Mawgan said again pointing again to Tamasine and himself "have to keep you hidden for a day or two do you understand"

Again Ramjam just nodded.

"I don't know if he understands English" Tamasine said as she stood beside Mawgan.

Ramjam again nodded as if to say yes he did.

"Do you understand that we will not heart you, we want to help you". Tamasine said as she sat back down on the bed beside him.

"Yes" came the reply.

"Are you hungry" Mawgan asked.

"Where's the French man". Ramjam asked in perfect English. He was holding the soars on his wrest.

18

Tamasine put her arm around him. "The French man has gone; we took you off his ship". She said as she gently rubbed his forehead as you would a child.

"My name is not Ramjam, that bloody French man called me Ramjam". The Indian replied now not looking quite so scared.

"What is your name". Tamasine asked quietly.

"My name is Rajah". He replied as if he was proud of it.

"Well Rajah we rescued you, because the French man said they were going to hang you". Mawgan said as if he was trying to make some excuse for what they had done.

"Better I do hang I have no life without my Annabel". Rajah replied.

"No man should hang for the love of a woman". Mawgan said firmly.

Tamasine put her arm around Rajah. "You never know what the future holds you will meet her again I'm sure of it". She said as she smiled sweetly at him.

"That won't happen her Father sent her out there to marry the Governor General's son, he is". Rajah paused then continued. "How you say he is a twerp". She will never love him" Rajah's eyes started to moisten.

"Is the marriage arranged?" Mawgan asked.

"Rupert the Governor General's son has gone to America to fight and they are to marry next year on his return" Rajah replied.

"Are you sure it's you she really loves, and you just weren't a bit of fun in his absence". Mawgan asked as he thought no one could resist a bit of excitement with a woman.

"I'm sure she hates him and his Father, I'm afraid she will kill herself before she marries him". Rajah was quite forceful as he said it.

Tamasine looked at Mawgan. "You think people jump in to bed with anyone just for the fun of it, it's time you realised what love means". She was really angry.

"I do love you even if you won't have me in your bed and I couldn't bear it if you went to another man I think I would kill myself". Mawgan went over to the bed and pulled her up as he said it.

"My Mawgan I believe you mean it". Tamasine replied as she put her arms around him and cuddled him.

"Now what about you Rajah my friend what are we going to do with you, we need some ware for you to stay whilst we sort out your future". Mawgan said as he put his arms around Tamasine.

Tamasine gave Mawgan a big hug as she replied. "I think he should stay with Willy he could help him with his pigs and odd jobs you are always given him too much to do".

"That's a good idea but I don't think I give him too much to do". Mawgan went over to Rajah. "I will do all I can to get your true love back to you". He said.

"You are a big old sentimental really what a pity you can't just keep it in your pants". Tamasine said as she kissed Mawgan on the cheek.

"I don't know what you mean". Mawgan paused and then said. "If you bring Rajah down later I will go and get Willy prepared.

Chapter 4

A couple of weeks had passed since the rescue of Rajah. He had moved in with Willy, Mawgan had to bribe him with sixpence so he could have an evening at Lowenna's. But he could have probably saved his money as Lowenna had a soft spot for Willy she would have bathed him for free.

It was now a hot summer's day and Tamasine had come up with a new way of teasing Mawgan, she would slip down to the bay and get slowly undressed, she knew Mawgan was watching her she would slowly remove her cloths first facing him then turning her back so all he ever saw was her back. She would run in to the sea and swim her body would twist and turn like a mermaid; she would always place her cloths on a rock so that when she came out of the water the lower part of her body was hid from view by the rock this happened ever day.

But on a bright morning as Tamasine was leaving her cottage for her swim she was meet by a little boy he couldn't have been more than five or six, he was dressed in rags no shoes just hessian wrapped around his feet. "Have you seen my father" he asked in a voice that was very polite but full of sorrow.

"No I'm afraid I've seen no strangers" Tamasine replied knowing that the little boy wasn't form the village.

"Would it be possible for you to give me something to eat"? The boy asked still sounding very polite.

"Of course" Tamasine replied as she crooked down in front of him.

"It's not for me it's for my sister Miss!!" The boy replied as he ran back the road a little way and picked up a little girl that he had laid at the bottom of a hedge.

Tamasine had followed him back to her. "Is this your sister"? She asked as she took the little girl from him, the little girl was in quite some state, dressed in rags her legs covered in what should be in a nappy, of which she had none. I think you should come in doors and we can see what we can do.

Tamasine feed them and had taken the dirty clothes off the little girl and was now giving her a bath, as she was bathing her she asked the little boy. "Where have you come from"?

"Bodmin". The little boy replied.

"You have walked from Bodmin!!!" Tamasine found it hard to believe what she was hearing.

"Yes". The boy replied. "Will you help me find my father?" He asked.

"I will do my best what's his name" Tamasine asked.

"I don't know". The boy replied with the saddest of faces.

With that the door opened "Tamasine are you all right" a voice said "I missed you this morning".

Tamasine new right away it was Mawgan'. "What do you mean you missed me"? She replied.

Mawgan walked in to the room. "Well your swim of course". He had a smirk on his face.

"What you mean have you been watching me". She replied trying to sound surprised.

"Of course I have never seen such beauty". He replied with a grin as wide as Penzance harbour.

"When where you last in Bodmin". Tamasine asked sarcastically.

"Bodmin". Mawgan paused. "Why"? He asked

"Because this pair are looking for their Father". Tamasine said as she stood aside so Mawgan could see the children.

Before he could answer the little boy ran over. "Is this my father"? He asked pulling at Mawgan's shirt.

"I don't think so dear". Tamasine said wishing she hadn't joked about it when she saw the look of disappointment on his face.

"Where's their mother". Mawgan asked as he bent down and picked the boy up.

"I don't know I haven't got that far yet the boy speaks as if they are well to do". Tamasine was quite taken in by the boy's manners.

"The men took her". The little boy replied as he started to cry.

"What men". Mawgan asked as he put the boy down beside Tamasine.

"The men said she stole some cheese from farmer Richards". The little boy said as he put his arm around Tamasine's leg.

Mawgan looked deep in thought and then he suddenly announced. "Looks like a trip to Bodmin tomorrow". He turned and started to make his way to the door.

"What about the children" Tamasine asked.

Mawgan turned and put his hand in his pocket. "They will have to stay with you until tomorrow." He handed two gold coins to Tamasine. "Better go down Maggie Rowes and get some cloths." He said as he turned and went out the door.

"Thanks." She replied with a smile.

When Mawgan had gone Tamasine spent some time trying to find out more about the children, the boy she learned was called Arthur and the little girl Amy. Their mother was called Victoria and they lived on a farm and the farmer was called Mr Richards. She them went down to Maggie Rowe's shop to get some clothes and shoes.

They looked like completely different children, and that afternoon she took them down to Mawgan's. "Is that the sea?" Arthur asked full of excitement as they got to the cliffs above Mawgan's house.

"Yes dear that's the sea!!!" Tamasine replied as she could see the excitement on Arthur's face.

"Then that's where my Father is". Arthur jumped up towards his sister who Tamasine was carrying. "We have found him". He shouted.

Mawgan heard all the excitement and came out to meet them. "What's all the excitement"? He asked.

"It's Arthur he has seen the sea and thinks his Father is here". She replied knowing that Arthur was going to be disappointed.

"It would seem that he is a sea going fell-a then". Mawgan said as he scratched his chin.

"Well that doesn't narrow it down much dose it". Tamasine said as she lifted the little girl higher up on her shoulder.

Mawgan led them in to his cottage, he them opened the door that led out into the garden overlooking the bay. "Is your father on a boat"? He asked Arthur as he lifted him up on to the hammock that was tied between two trees.

"I think so Mother said he had gone to see". Arthur said in a grown up way.

Mawgan pushed him back and fro in the hammock. "You are very forward for your age". Mawgan then paused, before asking. "How old are you".

"I'm six and Amy is three, Mother said I was a little man and had to act like one". Arthur replied quite proudly.

"And when did she say this". Mawgan asked.

"When the men took her away". He replied.

Mawgan wanted to find out more about the farmer were his Mother worked and where they lived and what there surname was, it appeared that they lived in a house at the bottom of a field on the farm and there surname was Pringle.

"I don't think the children should come to Bodmin tomorrow". Mawgan said to Tamasine.

"Who will we get to look after them" Tamasine asked looking surprised.

"You can". Mawgan replied.

Tamasine sat Amy on the bottom of the hammock. "I'm going with you". She replied.

Mawgan thought for a moment. "It's a long ride; it will be a long day". He said.

"I don't care how long it is, if this pair can walk it I'm sure I can ride it". Tamasine replied with a look on her face that told Mawgan her mind was made up.

"Ok we will get Willy and Rajah to look after them". Mawgan couldn't help smiling as he thought of that pair looking after them.

"Is that wise". Tamasine asked, she then looked around. "Where are they" she asked as there was no sign of ether Willy or Rajah.

"They will be back dreakly they have gone to meet a ship, the Prussia Prince she is laden with tea silks and cottons". Mawgan put his telescope I can just see them coming around the Mount let's hope they have spent my ten pounds wisely". He said.

"Let's hope they spent it all on silks". Tamasine said with a smile.

Mawgan smiled back. "I think you should go just in case the custom men come around, I will sort out everything for tomorrow but we will have to leave at six". Mawgan said as he lifted the children of the hammock.

"That's fine I think I will ask Winnie Treewin if she will look in on Willy and Rajah tomorrow, just to make sure they are all right". Tamasine new she had to swallow her pride where Winnie was concerned. She picked up Amy and then caught hold of Arthur's hand and made her way up to Winnie's.

Chapter 5

The next morning at six AM Mawgan was up at Tamasine's with two horses all saddled up. Willy and Rajah were with him to look after the children. "The children are still a sleep". Tamasine said as she opened the door. "Now don't you pair go frightening them mind".

Tamasine was dressed in a silk low cut blouse a pair of britches that where tight around the bottom and belled out around the knees and a pair of boots that came just below the knee.

"You *add-en* better trot something could come bouncing out". Willy paused then continued. "What do *E* think *Cap'n*"?

"Lilly-Rose always said there was an Angele amongst us". He replied as he found it hard to take his eyes of her.

"You can look as much as you like but trust me there will be no touching". Tamasine was still teasing Mawgan.

Tamasine passed Mawgan a sheep skin coat which he took and rolled up. "It's rather hot I don't think you will need it". He said as he strapped it behind the saddle on one of the horses.

"I fear for the horses this whether" Tamasine said as she stood on the low wall outside the cottage and mounted one of them.

"We won't be able to work them hard, it will be a long day" Mawgan said as he mounted his horse.

Tamasine turned to Willy "Remember what I said don't frighten those children when they wake up". She said. "Winnie will be up soon". She shouted as they trotted off down the lane.

They made steady progress to Bodmin they made the horses trot a while, then slowed them down to cool at a walking pace, they arrived in Bodmin around ten AM Mawgan thought it better if they found the farmer, Mawgan could pay him then perhaps they could get the women out of gaol if that is where she was.

After asking around they made their way up a long track. Where they were met by a man with a pitch fork over his shoulder. "What do you want he said angrily"?

"Would you be farmer Richard's". Mawgan asked.

"I what of it". Came the reply.

"I believe you had a Victoria Pringle work for you". Mawgan said as he dismounted his horse.

"I". Came the reply.

"Do you know where we could find her"? Mawgan asked as he came around the front of the horse.

"I". Again was the reply.

Tamasine had dismounted from her horse that was drinking from a small pool that had been made in a stream that ran down beside the tack. "You paying for that". The man asked firmly.

"We will pay you". Mawgan said quite calmly. "Now tell me my friend I believe Victoria stole from you". He said still calmly.

"What of it". The man again replied, he had a long strand of hay in his mouth which fell out when he spoke.

"I would like to pay you for what she stole, and I would like to get her out of gaol so she can go to her children". Mawgan said as he took a hessian bag tied at the top out of his pocket. Taking two gold coins out of the bag will this cover it and the water"? He asked as his horse was now drinking.

"I". The man said as he took the coins from Mawgan.

"How do we get her out of gaol"? Tamasine asked, she had been silent up to now she thought the man very rude.

"I will go and see Lord Tremeldon and tell him you paid, and see if he will except the fact that you paid me, after all it was his idea". The man said as he put the pitch fork that was over his shoulder in to the ground and leaned on it.

"How do you mean his idea!!"? Mawgan asked. Idea about what he thought.

"I didn't worry about a bit of milk or cheese; I knew she was doing it for the kids". The man paused and spat out the corner of his mouth. "When Lord Tremeldon came up here he saw her taking some cheese. I told him no worry it's just for the kids". The man's voice changed as he looked up at Tamasine with what looked like a tear in his eye.

"So what was the problem"? Tamasine asked the rudeness had completely gone from the man.

"Lord Tremeldon told me I had to press charges against her; otherwise every employee would be doing it". The man said as he leaned forward and pated Tamasine's horse on the neck.

"Surely you could have said you didn't mind". Mawgan said sounding now quite angry.

"If Lord Tremeldon's your landlord you can't say no, he would through me off the farm, in fact he made that quite clear". The man said.

"Well we will go to the gaol and see what we can do; did she go up in front of the clearage"? Mawgan asked as he held his hand out for the man to shake.

The man shook his hand and handed him his coins back. "I don't want your money". He said. And as for the church they would have no say Lord Tremeldon is the only law around here. I haven't heard what happened I never leave the farm". The man picked up the rains of Tamasine's horse and handed them too her and asked. "Would you like to see where she lived"?

"I think we would". Tamasine replied thinking if she got some of the children's clothes they could somehow take their mother back with them.

The man pointed to a shack that was a little further up the track. "I'll have to leave you now" He said as he put the pitch fork back over his shoulder and walked on down the track.

Mawgan and Tamasine led their horses up towards the shack. "You looked as if you know this Lord Tremeldon". Tamasine said as they got to the shack and tied the horses to a branch on the hedge.

"Everyone in Cornwall knows Lord Tremeldon his fingers are in everything all the mines and shipping, god knows how much land he owns, there is not a man in business in Cornwall that hasn't come across him. Mawgan paused as he opened the door of the shack. "O and that includes me". He continued. "My ships work for the bastard".

They were now inside it was quite small and the smell of wood smoke was in abundance even though no fire was lit, Tamasine looked through the cloths but nothing she thought was worth taking. "Come on" Mawgan said. "Let's get down to the gaol".

Just as they were about to leave Mawgan noticed a letter on a shelf above the mantelpiece, he picked it up it was unopened and addressed to Victoria Pringle. "Do you think I should open it"? He said taping the envelope on his hand.

Tamasine looked at it. "Its good writing it might be something important that will get her out of gaol".

Mawgan opened the letter and started to read it, then. "Bloody hell!!" Came out of his lips.

"What is it"? Tamasine asked with the look of anxiousness on her face.

Mawgan read her the letter.

My Darling Victoria.

I have been unable to see you as my fleet is preparing to sail to America. We are to take red coats there to help stop the rebellion that is happening out there.

I'm not sure how long I will be away and our baby will be born before I return.

I have told Damaris that I will not be returning to her. We both know the marriage was wrong and a scam by her father. So my darling we can spend the rest of our lives together with are beautiful son and baby that will be born when I return as this will be my last trip.

You have always refused my money but now you know I have left my wife use the money below to get us a house, and look after yourself and children until I return this should be more than adequate.

All my love my dearest.

Henry

PS I have informed the bank and they will open an account for you. Take this note with you when you go and see him.

Mawgan read out from another piece of paper.

To Jonathan Brute the manager of the bank of Truro please release the sum of three thousand ponds from my account and pay it to Miss Victoria Pringle of Bodmin.

Signed this day the twenty sixth of November seventeen hundred and seventy three.

Admiral Sir Henry Richard Penrose.

Mawgan folded the letter up and put it back in the envelope

"How sad she had no need to steel". Tamasine said she had a tear in her eye.

"This was written nearly four years ago Amy must be his". Mawgan said as he put his arm around Tamasine.

"I wonder why she never opened it It's been there for four years". Tamasine said as she put her arm around Mawgan for a little comfort.

"Let's get down to the gaol and get her out then we will have all the answers". Mawgan said as he led Tamasine over to the door.

They mounted their horses and rode down to the gaol where they were met by a man of about forty; he was as scruffy as anyone could be, he just had two over large teeth one on each side of his mouth, his head was sort of held to one side, almost as if he couldn't move it, Tamasine was very nervous as they approached him. "I'd like to see who's in charge please". Mawgan said as they demounted from their horses.

"That'll be me". The man replied as he put a clay pipe in his mouth.

"I have paid for the goods that it was alleged Victoria Pringle stole and now we would like her released". Mawgan said with a tone of authority.

"Bit difficult that would be". The man replied as he removed his pipe from his mouth and spat on the floor.

"How do you mean". Mawgan thought it would be just a formality.

"She was hung yesterday". The man said it so calmly.

"How do you mean hung, you can't be hung over a piece of cheese". Mawgan replied angrily.

"You can in Bodmin when Lord Tremeldon says so". The man said as once more he put the pipe in his mouth and drew hard on it trying not to show any emotion.

"How can you do this job". Tamasine asked angrily.

"I just do my job I might-en like what happens sometimes but I got a women and kids to feed". You could tell the man was upset by what had happened even though trying hard not to show it.

"Where do I find Lord Tremeldon" Mawgan asked.

"He lives at Fawn House you take the Camborn road and a mile out you will see the big gates leading up to the house". The man held his hand out for Mawgan to shake as he said it, he shook it as if he was trying to offer some sort of apology for what had happened.

The pair of them mounted up and cantered all the way until they came up to the gates of Fawn house. Tamasine had a job to keep up she could tell Mawgan was seething, she had never seen him like this. Mawgan leaned forward and opened the gate they rode up a long gravel drive which opened up into a large court yard in front of a large country house, they dismounted, and tied up the horses and made their way to a large oak door, Mawgan banged on it hard. After a few moments the door opened and a man dressed in a morning suit opened the door. "Can I help you". He asked.

"We would like to see Lord Tremeldon" Mawgan replied.

"Who shall I say is calling". The man asked.

"Mawgan, Captain Mawgan". Came the reply.

The man left and returned a few minutes later. "My Lord is unavailable to day, if it's regarding shipping contracts you should contact your agent". The man said. He turned to shut the door.

Mawgan pushed it wide open and stormed in Tamasine followed close behind "Tremeldon!!!" He shouted with rage in his voice, they stormed down through a large hall and pushed open a double door at the end of the hall, in what seemed to be a large library. Standing by the window was a man with a multicolour silk gown on "are you Tremeldon" Mawgan shouted.

"Lord Tremeldon" the man replied.

"You had a women hung for stealing a piece of cheese" Mawgan again shouted this time his face was just inches from the Lords.

"And what concern is that of yours". Lord Tremeldon asked as he nervously took a couple of paces backwards.

"The children they concern me". Mawgan replied, for every pace backwards the Lord took Mawgan took one forward.

"Why are you so concerned about a couple of bastard kids"? The Lord asked with a tone of couldn't care less in his voice.

"Bastard's are they what if I was to tell you there father is an Admiral". Mawgan said with an air of cockiness.

"What do you know of that". The Lord asked surprisingly.

"I have a letter in my hand that proves it". Mawgan took the letter out of his pocket and waved it in front of Lord Tremeldon who tried to grab it.

"That Admiral you talk of is married to my daughter". The Lord replied angrily.

"O so this is what it's all about Henry left your daughter for Victoria and you couldn't stand it so you murdered her". Mawgan said calmly.

"He and my daughter were to part they both say they had found love else ware. My daughter with a peasant and him with that slut. How could he love that slut before my daughter". Lord Tremeldon sat down and put his head in his hands.

"I can't believe you had her killed for love, and why now he told your daughter four years ago". Mawgan was trying to understand.

"I had her hung for steeling and that's the punishment for the crime and that's an end to it". Lord Tremeldon stood up. "As for the other I only found out two weeks ago. I had some news that Admiral Henry Penrose was killed in a battle of the Americas". He paused then continued. "I went to tell my daughter it was then that she told me she wanted to go to that Pringle woman and tell her but I forbid it".

Mawgan again started to get angry. "So you went to her place of work and got her arrested and then you past the death penalty on her". Mawgan turned away and then turned again to face him. "In my book that's cold bloody murder and if I can find a way for you to pay I will". Mawgan turned to Tamasine "Come on let's get out of here".

"That's the different between me and you I can make the rules to suit myself, and people like you have to obey them". Lord Tremeldon chuckled as they started to leave the room.

Mawgan stopped turned went back and pulled a punch he hit the Lord hard in the face blood spouted out of his nose.

"You'll pay for that" Lord Tremeldon shouted as he staggered to his feet with Mawgan and Tamasine leaving the room.

They made their way to their horses. "You shouldn't have done that" Tamasine said "He might get you hung" Tamasine had never seen Mawgan like this he was always so calm whatever the provocation.

"He wouldn't dare" Mawgan replied with a smile.

"What are we going to tell that poor little boy" Tamasine asked.

"The truth, that's the only thing we can do". Mawgan replied as they rode of down the drive.

"I still don't understand why she never opened that letter" Tamasine said as she got up alongside Mawgan.

"I think that's simple I doubt she could read". Mawgan dug his hells in to his horse as if to let out a bit of anger.

Chapter 6

It was late when they returned to Tamasine's cottage, Tamasine went in and to her surprise there was no one there. Mawgan had left to take the horses down to his stable. Tamasine ran down to his cottage and opened the door, lying on the floor fast asleep was Amy cuddled in to Rajah and Arthur cuddled in to Willy. Her face just lit up, it was only a few moments before Mawgan arrived the pair of them just stood in the door way and smiled. They quietly stepped outside the stars where shining and the moon was lighting the whole place up, you could hear the waves down in the cove. Mawgan slowly put his arm around Tamasine as they stood on the edge of the garden looking down in to the cove. "That's where you swim". He said as he pointed to a rock on the corner of the beach.

Tamasine looked up at him and smiled. "I don't believe you ever saw me". She replied knowing full well he did.

"O trust me I did the most beautiful site I ever saw". Mawgan's face was getting closer to hers as he said it.

Tamasine didn't move and it wasn't long before they were in a long passionate kiss. Mawgan brought his hand up and cupped one of her breasts. Tamasine put her arms around him and pulled him in to her body as close as she could, then suddenly she stopped and pushed him a way. "NO!!" she shouted.

"What is it, what's the matter"? Mawgan asked with a note of surprise.

"I know what would happen, and I've told you many times". Tamasine paused and caught hold of Mawgan's hand then continued. "You're a good man and I love you more than a woman could love any man but I won't share you with other women". She squeezed his hand tightly as she said it.

"I promise you if you will be mine I will never look at another woman". Mawgan said as he turned Tamasine around to face him.

"It's not the looking that troubles me; I know I would just be a play thing for a week or two. But then you would never turn the opportunity down with other women. You just can't resist hoisting your main sale at every opportunity". Tamasine said as she stretched up and kissed him on the cheek.

They were soon interrupted by Willy coming out the cottage door. "*You-m* back then". He said with a yawn.

"How have the children been" Tamasine asked with some concern.

"No problem what you left them to eat was fine, bloody pity you didn't tell us about the little maids *tother* end" Willy said with a smile.

"O did you manage that all right" Tamasine hoped they had.

"No problem I left that end to Rajah". Willy replied with a grin as Rajah came to join them.

Mawgan was just telling them about their day when Arthur the little boy came out holding the hand of his sister. "Have you got my mother"? He asked looking around.

"I'm afraid not". Tamasine said as she bent down and picked the little girl up.

Arthur sat down on the grass. "Well I will just have to find my father now wont I". He said in a determined voice for a young boy.

"We have some news about your father, and I'm afraid it's not good" Mawgan said as he sat down on the grass beside him and put his arm around him.

"You're going to tell me he is dead aren't you". Arthur said with the tone in his voice full of sadness, it was like as if he knew.

"Yes I'm afraid he is and I have to tell you your mother is as well". Mawgan thought it better to get it all out now.

Arthur started to cry when Amy said. "What's dead"?

"Dead is something that happens to all of us one day". Tamasine said as she sat down on the grass with Amy, on the other side of Arthur.

"What happens when we die" Arthur asked.

Tamasine moved so that she could sit little Amy between her legs and put an arm around Arthur, "We go to heaven if we are good" she said.

35

"Where's heaven" Amy asked as she turned her head backwards and looked at Tamasine.

Tamasine pointed to the stars that where shining so bright. "Every twinkling little star is a heaven and that's where we go when we die". Tamasine said.

"Will my mother and father be on the same star"? Arthur asked with a puzzled look.

"O yes your mother and father will be together forever". Tamasine said as she gave him a little hug.

"I don't know what we do now do we go back to mothers house. Will I have to help farmer Richards". Arthur sounded so grown up.

"You won't be able to go back there as there is no one there to look after you". Mawgan explained.

"I could work for farmer Richards and look after Amy". Arthur said quite proudly.

This was a five year old thinking like a twenty year old no one could believe their ears. Each one of them had a tear in their eye. They were all getting so attached to the children.

"I think you should stay with me" Tamasine said as she pulled Amy up on to her lap.

"I have to work" Arthur said "you will need us to pay our way mother always said no one can hurt you if you pay your way".

The tear in Mawgan's eye started to roll down his cheek as he said "You can work for me I need a good man". What a proud woman their mother must have been he thought.

"That's settled then". Tamasine said. "Now we must all go and get some sleep".

They all returned to their respective cottages.

A couple of weeks had passed and every morning Arthur would run down to Mawgan's like a man going to work. Mawgan would give him little errands to run and Arthur was being admired by all around. Winnie Trewin and Tamasine started to grow closer by their love for Amy this was one person they could both love. There feuds over Mawgan had been put to one side, in fact Mawgan was being a little neglected in all of this. Tamasine and Winnie had been down on the quay with Amy on their return they stopped and talked to Lilly-Rose. "Trouble brewing for Mawgan". She warned.

"What trouble"? Tamasine asked.

"Trouble on two fronts". She replied with a worried look.

"Will he be all right"? Tamasine asked she didn't like the look on Lilly-rose's face.

"I see a lot of adventure, a lot of heart ache, a lot of crying, but I can't see the ending but you both play your part". Lilly-Rose put her hand out and caught hold of Tamasine's and lightly pated her on the wrist as she continued. "And you dear your part will be far more than you could ever have imagined".

"How do you mean". Tamasine asked with the look of bewilderment.

"I don't know I see know more than I have said". Lilly-Rose replied as she let go of Tamasine's hand and put her clay pipe back in her mouth and drew hard on it.

They left Lilly-Rose and made their way back up to the cliff they parted at the fork in the top of the lane. As Tamasine thought she should go and see Mawgan to warn him of what Lilly-Rose had said.

Winnie returned to her cottage it was a hot summer's day, as she got to her cottage she noticed sat just along the lane was a man dressed in a white shirt with a large cravat around his neck, he was wearing tight white trousers with boots up to just below his knee. The sweet was running down his face, Winnie went and approached him. "Are you all right?" She asked.

"Do you live here"? The man replied.

"Yes"

"Then I wonder if I could trouble you for a drink". The man asked as he stood up.

"Of course you should come in out of the sun". Winnie turned and walked towards the gate.

The man quickly caught her up. "I would like to introduce myself" he said "I am James Wilmot Sparrow, a servant of his majesty King George the third and I am here on his business". He stood proud as he said it.

"O and what business would that be"? Winnie asked, she had a little giggle at the way the man introduced himself.

"To put an end to all the smuggling that goes on here". He replied with a note of authority.

"I don't think you will find any of that here Mr James Wilmot Sparrow". Winnie replied as she showed the man in to her cottage. "Now what can I get you to drink".

"A cup of tea would be nice". The man replied.

"I'm afraid I can't afford tea". Winnie said knowing the tea she had was smuggled. "I have some elderberry cordial, that's very refreshing".

"That will be fine thank you". The man replied.

"You want to be careful they say that it can be a bit of an aphrodisiac". Winnie said as she handed him the tankard with her charming smile.

The man blushed, he had a job to keep his eyes of her as most men did, she was full bodied with a beautiful face, and her low cut dress left very little to the imagination.

"Do you know a Captain Mawgan"? The man asked.

"Yes"

"I have been told he is a notorious smuggler and a proper villain"? The man looked stern as he said it.

Winnie laughed. "Well James Wilmot Sparrow where did you get that from"? She asked.

"I have a letter in my possession from his majesty parliament it is signed by the king". The man replied producing a letter from his pocket.

"Let me tell you James Wilmot Sparrow you your king and his parliament have got it wrong". Winnie said as she took the letter from him and pretended to read it.

God he thought she is beautiful, for a moment his mind was taking of smuggling, before he replied. "I will not judge a man until I know the facts our King has many outside influences and they do not all mean
38

well". The man looked quite sincere as he took the letter back from Winnie.

"Do you know James Wilmot Sparrow I think I believe you". Winnie said as she took the empty tankard from him.

"Where is there a place to have a bath and stay". James asked.

"You can have a bed at Lowanna's and they also have baths". Winnie paused and smiled. "You also get a few extras". She said still smiling.

"What extras"

"Extras that men seem to enjoy". Winnie could hold the giggle back no longer as she could see James now saw what she meant.

James gulped. "Is there anywhere else"? He asked nervously.

Winnie thought for a minute. "You could stay here I have my mother's room no one has slept there since she died but you are welcome". Winnie thought it better he staid where she could keep an eye on him. The words of Lilly-Rose where ringing through her head.

"I have an allowance of three pence a night which is to include breakfast if that is acceptable to you". James replied quite excitedly.

"That sounds fine now what about that bath". Winnie said as she turned and poked the fire and put some large lumps of coal on it then lifted two very large kettles and placed them on top.

"O I don't think I should bath now". James said quite nervously.

"O no worries I have to go out for a couple of hours you just make yourself at home". Winnie shouted from the kitchen as she hid the tea and made sure no other smuggled items were lying around.

Winnie pulled a large bath in from outside the back door to where the fire was burning, the room was very hot. "Now hear is your bath the water is on the fire there is a clean towel on that chair". Winnie pointed to a chair over by the window. "Now I'm off and I will see you latter". She said as she opened the door and left.

Winnie ran down the track to Mawgan's she couldn't wait to tell him about James Wilmot Sparrow.

Chapter 7

Mawgan was standing in the garden looking down to the cove where Tamasine and Amy were paddling in the water, Winnie noticed a troubled look on his face she had never seen him like this. "What is it she asked"? He looked like he had troubles without James Wilmot Sparrow adding to them.

"O nothing to worry you and our friends". He replied with a little smile that seemed a bit of an effort.

"That's why we are friends to share are troubles as well as everything else we share". Winnie said she put her arm around him.

"You tell me what brings you here ,and when Tamasine comes up I will tell you my troubles".

Winnie told him all about her visitor James Wilmot Sparrow and how he was going to stay with her so she could keep an eye on what he was doing.

"I suppose that means I won't be able to call". Mawgan said with a smile.

"He's not in my bed that space will always be for you". Winnie replied with a large grin.

Tamasine was making her way up from the beach she also knew something was amiss with Mawgan. Her and Amy made their way up over the last piece of cliff and in to the garden. "Has he told you what's wrong"? She shouted as she entered the garden, Winnie was looking as concerned as Tamasine.

"No". Winnie replied shaking her head.

"Sit down and I will tell you" Mawgan said as he sat on the edge of the hammock. My dear girls my business has come to an end". Mawgan was looking quite sad.

"How do you mean come to an end"? Tamasine asked both her and Winnie where looking puzzled.

"None of my ships will be loaded or unloaded at any Cornish Port". He replied.

"I don't understand why not". Winnie asked.

"There has been a lot of pressure put on the company's and owners that I work for. Someone who has as much influence as I thought he had". Mawgan replied as he looked at Tamasine his eyes full of sadness.

"I still don't understand who". Tamasine said quite forcefully.

"Lord bloody Tremeldon that's who Lord bloody Tremeldon!!!" Mawgan replied with anger in his voice.

"O God what are you going to do". Winnie asked as she sat down on the grass.

Tamasine sat down beside her. "O I'm not worried about myself, after all I'm quite well off, my ships have done me well. It's the crews. Where will they find work I can't see some of them going down the mine for a Penney or two an hour". Mawgan put his head in his hands as he said it.

"That's you all over its always other people never mind what it does to you, we all know it's not the money, those ships are your life you can't give them up just like that". Tamasine said angrily.

"I've made up my mind I won't fight it I will keep my biggest ship but the rest will go". Mawgan now looked a little more like himself.

"What are you going to do with yourself"? Tamasine asked.

"Spend my time wooing you". He replied with a smile.

"I'm being serious". Tamasine had a little smile as she rather liked the idea.

"Well I shall be away for six months when I go and get Rajah's women and then we will see". Mawgan replied with some conviction.

"How are you going to get her". Winnie asked.

"I don't know yet but I will put a plan together over the next few days". Mawgan said as he stood up and looked to the sky as if for inspiration.

"You're a good man Mawgan". Winnie said as she got up and kissed him on the cheek.

"Now I need you to go and keep your visitor out of the way tonight as we have a little business to attend to". Mawgan said as he gently kissed her on the cheek.

"I'll ask no questions". She said as she walked towards the gate.

"What visitor"? Tamasine asked.

"I'll explain". Mawgan said as Winnie left.

After Winnie had left Mawgan explained about Winnie's visitor whilst they both played with Amy on the grass like a married couple with their child.

"Will you let the children sleep here tonight?" Mawgan asked "I want to go out with Willy to meet a ship, and I would so much like you to be here when I return".

"Of course I'll be here". Tamasine replied she wanted to support Mawgan she knew how sad he was felling.

Mawgan just smiled at her as if to say thanks.

"I will take this pair of angles up to my place and give them there bath and tea, and will be down later;" Tamasine said. "What time you going out?"

"About nine I think we will take Rajah with us". Mawgan replied as he picked Amy up and swung her around.

Tamasine left with Arthur and Amy, once she had bathed and fed them she returned with them again just before nine.

Back at Winnie's cottage she was having difficulty stopping her visitor going out to find Mawgan. "I think I will have a walk along the cliffs, I might be able to see what this so called Captain Mawgan's up to". James said as he picked up his coat.

"I have a better idea James Wilmot Sparrow". Winnie replied knowing she had to keep him away tonight.

"What might that be"? James asked.

Winnie pulled her dress down hard so that she was showing a deep cleavage; she could see James was having difficulty to keep his eyes off her. "I suggest you come and sit beside me and I will tell you all about

Captain Mawgan, and then you can tell me all about James Wilmot Sparrow". Winnie patted the seat beside her as she said it.

James nervously put his coat down came and sat down beside her. James had a funny sort of charm about him that Winnie was beginning to find attractive.

"Tell me then everything you know about Captain Mawgan". James sat nervously down beside her.

"Where shall I start" Winnie paused then smiled. "When Mawgan was fifteen a ship carrying people being deported to the colonies hit the rocks just off the mount. It was a horrendous night people still say it was the worst storm ever seen. No one knew how that ship got so close to the shore wither it was blown there or the captain tried to go for shelter. No one went out to try and rescue it because they knew there was nothing of value on her. Except that is Mawgan and his Father, no one knows how many where on the ship or how many died, but the one thing that is known is that Mawgan and his Father rowed through the storm not once but three times, and saved twenty seven people. Unfortunately on the last trip Mawgan's father was washed overboard and never seen again".

"You're making it sound like he is some kind of hero". James said as he could see Winnie was getting emotional.

"I would say a saint as well as a hero, he was to me and my mother as we were the first ones rescued".

"What! You where on the ship?"

"Yes I was twelve at the time and we were being deported not knowing where we were going just because my father couldn't pay his rent, he died that night a broken man. The sight of him slowly slipping in to the water will live with me forever".

"You poor thing". James said as he put his arm around her as he could see how upset she was.

"My mother was cold as we all laid on the beach exhausted not knowing where to go when a lady Mrs Nancarrow came and brought us up to this cottage, and nursed my mother for days but she never got over it and died after a short while".

"I don't know what to say, what happened to you then". James was sounding very concerned.

"Me I just carried on living here, I don't even know who's cottage it is I have asked Mawgan lots of times and Tamasine Mrs Nancarrow's daughter, but they say they don't know".

"Did Mawgan's Father have many ships"? James asked.

"No he only had a fishing boat".

"So if Mawgan's not smuggling how has he so many ships at such a young age"? James was now back on to official questions.

"Determination and hard work a week after Mawgan's father died the ship was still lying of the mount Mawgan salvaged it repaired it and within six months he was sailing up to Wales to fetch coal for the foundry in Hale".

"It looks like my information might be wrong about the man to do that at such a young age is something special". James shuffled around in the seat, "Are you and him an item" he asked.

"Why no, we have had our moments but his heart lies else ware". Winnie replied with a smile. "Now James Wilmot Sparrow I will get us a drink and you can tell me all about you". Winnie got up and made her way to the kitchen, she returned with a flagon and two beakers, "its elderberry wine". She said as she pulled out the stopper and poured a beaker full for James and half as much for herself. "Now James lets here it all".

"Nothing much to tell my name is James Wilmot Sparrow and I am a servant of his majesty King George the third". James paused "O and yes I live with my Mother in Plymouth". James then sat right back in the seat and took a large drink from the beaker.

"Is that it". Winnie asked in a surprising voice. "There must be more!! What about a Mrs James Wilmot Sparrow or a girl friend or where you live".

"I have no girl friend or any interest in any, my work is all need".

"Everyone needs someone". Winnie replied as she toped up his beaker with some more elderberry wine.

"I don't all I am interested is stopping people from smuggling and avoiding paying his majesty and his government there dues". James again paused and took another drink from the beaker before continuing. "Do you know we are fighting wars so that we can hold on to our colonies? Are red coats are engaged in fierce battles across the Americas, much money is needed to support this. Every one that smuggles goods is depriving our country of this much needed money and they should hang".

Winnie took a big gulp of her drink when James mentioned the word hang, "I think that's a bit severe". She replied.

"You think so why should they live when our red coats are being slathered". James was now talking with a mixture of drink and angry.

"I don't think we should be out there fighting anyway we have people here that our so poor they can't feed their families and we are spending money on things that our thousands of miles away many of us don't even know where they are". Winnie was now as mad as James was.

"It is a good job men make decisions". James said as his face changed to a smile.

"And what do you think women should do". Winnie asked sarcastically.

James went red and sounded embarrassed as he said. "Their job is reproduction".

Winnie started to tease him. "And how do they do that". She asked getting herself as close to him as she could.

"I think I should get to bed and have an early night as I want to check the area out tomorrow". James stuttered as he drank the last drop of his drink. "Are you still up to showing me around"? He asked.

"Of course". She replied as she stood up and bent over James to pick up his beaker, she could see his eyes peering down her cleavage.

James got up and went on to bed. Winnie washed up the beakers and tidied the place up a little before she made her way to bed. The bed rooms where opposite separated by a very narrow passage way there were no doors just a curtain across the opening. Winnie went to her room she could see there was a large gap in the curtain across James's room she could see him in bed facing her room, she could see he closed his eyes and pretended to be asleep when she looked through the gap. Winnie went in to her room and tried to pull the curtain something she had never done as she lived on her own. The curtain would only move a short distance leaving the whole room fully exposed to James opposite. Winnie smiled to herself as she knew James would be watching as she slowly and in a teasing way got undressed. She slowly folded back the bed cloths before getting in, standing in the doorway completely naked yet showing nothing in an elegant way.

Chapter 8

Down at Captain Mawgan's the night had been spent bringing in a large shipment of contraband. Mawgan had bought more contraband than he had ever bought before, this summed up the sort of man he was if he was going away for a few months he didn't want his local people to go without and by selling contraband he would completely feed some families. Willy and Rajah had spent the whole night storing it in a secret cave that went back under the cliff it was reached by a long stone stair case which was behind the fireplace in Mawgan's cottage. Mawgan was now going to concentrate on his trip to free Rajah's girl.

Tamasine was down to Mawgan's early with Arthur and Amy she wanted to talk to Mawgan about the letter Henry Penrose had written to Victoria the children's mother. If he had arranged for their mother to have some money then surely this should go to the children in some form of trust.

"That has been on my mind too". Mawgan said after Tamasine had spoken to him.

"How do we approach the situation? We know Lord Tremeldon will stop it from happening somehow". Tamasine said with a big sigh.

"I think we should go and see Henry Penrose's wife, after all you never know she might be quite human". Mawgan picked Amy up and swung her around as he said it.

"Well if anyone can charm her you can". Tamasine replied with a smile.

"I don't know what you mean". Mawgan was still swinging Amy around who was enjoying every minute of it.

"I mean you could charm the tail of a mermaid". Tamasine said with a smile as she lifted Arthur up on to the hammock in the garden and started to push him to and fro.

Mawgan put his arm around Tamasine and whispered in her ear "You are the only mermaid for me and I haven't charmed the tail of you yet".

Tamasine tuned towards him kissed him on the cheek, and then gave Amy a kiss who he was holding in his arms.

Suddenly there was a shout from the gate way. "Anyone at home!!"? It was Winnie with more of a warning shout because normally she would just walk straight in.

"Over here". Mawgan replied in a tone that meant all is well.

Winnie and her visitor came over to where the others where all standing. "I would like to introduce you to James Wilmot Sparrow a loyal servant to King George the Third". Winnie said almost as if she was taking the mike as she introduced them all individually even the children.

"Are these your children?" James asked Mawgan.

"No they were made homeless by one of King George the thirds loyal servants". Mawgan replied quite sarcastically.

"How do you mean"? He asked"

Tamasine butted in quite angrily and told James all about Lord Tremeldon and how he had their mother hung.

"It is through Lord Tremeldon that your name has reached parliament, they intern have asked the men of Plymouth to put a stop to your antics, and it is them, the men of Plymouth that have sent me with the kings official blessing." James replied as took the letter from the king out of his pocket. But was this Captain Mawgan the notorious smuggler he was led to believe.

"Are you a lawyer?" Tamasine asked James.

"I am of sorts, I have studded the law very closely I needed to for my Job". He replied.

Tamasine then explained about the letter that they had found and how they thought the children might be entitled to the money.

"I don't think so in law". James replied, "A petty she didn't draw the money then they would have been, but it is a letter of intent to give, which was to their mother and not the children".

"But it was for the children's benefit and after all they are his children". Mawgan said as he again whizzed Amy around.

"The problem you have there, is the mother has never said weather they where or not". James was now sounding like a lawyer and it was quite obvious he knew what he was talking about. "If Lord Tremeldon is such a rouge as you make him to be, he only has to pay someone to say they went with the Mother and who is there to deny it. Lord Tremeldon is held in high esteem with the people of Plymouth".

"I think he would do that". Tamasine said, she then went on to explain that Mawgan and her where thinking of going to see Henry Penrose's wife. She also told him how Mawgan's ships could no longer load and discharge at any Cornish or Devon port.

"I have never meet Lord Tremeldon but do know he is a very influential figure both in Cornwall and in government". James replied.

"We meet him" Tamasine said with the note of excitement, "Mawgan gave him a bloody nose".

"That was probably a big mistake". James replied.

"I know that now, and whatever the wrongs he has done violence doesn't put it right I'm not proud of myself." Mawgan wanted James to know it was out of character.

Out through the door of Mawgan's cottage Willy and Rajah appeared, Winnie first introduced Willy. "This is Willy he was on the same ship as me and was also rescued by Mawgan and his Father".

James held out his hand and shook it, and then turned to Rajah. "And this is" He asked knowing in his mind who it was, as the talk of Devon and Cornwall was that the French man had lost his Indian prisoner in Penzance bay.

Mawgan quickly interrupted. "This is". He started to say, when James butted in,

"I am not here to find any fugitive I'm solely here to catch you smuggling". He said to Mawgan with a smile as he shook Rajah's hand.

Mawgan walked over to Winnie and whispered in her ear. "This James fellow doesn't seem a bad sort of chap".

"I find him quite sweet". She replied.

"When should we go to Bodmin" Tamasine asked Mawgan.

"That depends on Winnie if she will look after the children tomorrow then we can go then. It will be a long day as I have a little business in Falmouth so we will have to go that way". Mawgan said as he put his hand on Winnie's shoulder.

"I would like to help with that if it's ok". James said as he went over and pushed Arthur who was still lying in the hammock, he seemed to be quite taken back by this little community.

"That's fine". Winnie replied. "Now come on James I will take you around and introduce you to the rest of our little hamlet".

The pair of them left, Winnie felt quite proud of herself as she took James around to meet the village folk they were all a bit sceptical of James. It was clear they all had nothing but praise for Captain Mawgan and Preacher Jack said he didn't think god would approve of what James was doing.

They arrived at the seat where Lilly-Rose was sitting. Before Winnie could introduce James, Lilly-Rose had eyed him up and down. "*You'm* an official sort of bloke". She said.

"That's right". Winnie replied. "This is James Wilmot Sparrow a servant of King George the Third".

Lilly-Rose still eyeing him up and down. "I'm not sure if you are welcome or not". She said it was unusual for her not to be sure about something.

"How do you mean". Winnie asked.

Lilly- Rose caught hold of Winnie's hand and said. "Well I see a troubled sole, I see man torn between duty and love, and I can't see if love or duty wins".

"I don't understand what you mean". Winnie said with a worried look.

Lilly-Rose turned towards James still holding Winnie's hand. "How loyal are you to our King". She asked.

"As loyal as any man could be". He replied.

"If you had to choose between the love of a women, or duty to the King which would you chose". Lilly-Rose asked she still had Winnie's hand held tightly.

"The situation will never arise as I have no intentions of falling in love and I will always be loyal to the King". James replied with real conviction in his voice.

Lilly-Rose laughed "I know where your loyalties will be now". She said as she held Winnie's hand even tighter. "There might be some trouble but things will be all right". She whispered

"Lily-Rose I haven't a clue what you are talking about". Winnie said with a smile.

"You will one day when a choice has to be made". Lily-Rose replied her wrinkled face screwed up with a smile.

Winnie still confused looked at James. "Come on I will introduce you to Lowenna you never know you might find unexpected love there". Winnie caught hold of James hand and started to skip down the road.

The pair of them went down to Lowenna's where they were met by Lowenna and a couple of her girls. "I'll give him a bath". One of them said as she eyed James up and down.

"No he's mine". The other one said.

"Be quite the pair of you". Lowenna said. "If anyone gives him a bath it will be me"

James went quite red. "I don't need a bath thank you". He replied in a polite sort of way.

"Shame are you sure I can't persuade you". Lowenna put her large arms around James and pulled him in to her bosom.

They hadn't been there long before Willy arrived smelling strongly of pigs. "What you been up to". Winnie asked. "You are stinking".

Lowenna smiled. "I think he does it on purpose, he knows Mawgan will give him money for a bath" she said as she held her nose.

"I bet none of the girls will get in with him". Winnie said with a laugh.

"We put him in the bath and make him smell good, then we put him in another and then he's all mine I won't let any of my girl's have him. No I can give him the entire treat he needs".

James looked quite astonished. "You mean the girls actually bath the customers". He said.

"You seem surprised". Lowenna said. "You should try it someday you might enjoy it".

"Never" James replied firmly.

Lowenna laughed loudly. "If you change your mind I will bath you". She shouted as James and Winnie turned to walk back up the lane.

The rest of the day was spent with Winnie showing James around the place taking him everywhere that she knew no contraband had been landed.

Chapter 9

The next morning Tamasine brought the children up early to Winnie's; James was not yet out of bed. "He looks quite handsome don't you think". Winnie said as she pulled Tamasine over to look through the curtain where he was fast asleep.

"I do think he has a funny sort of charm". She whispered in reply.

Tamasine left the children and made her way down to Mawgan's where he was waiting with their horses all saddled up. In a matter of moments they where mounted up and on their way. There first stop was to be the docks in Falmouth where one of Mawgan's ships the Kernow Mist was tied up.

They were met by a man in a suit and large hat. "I shouldn't be dealing with you". He said as he shook Mawgan by the hand.

"O and why not". Mawgan asked.

"Been told if your ship is in my dock next week I'll get no more government work". He replied.

"I better take her somewhere else then". Mawgan said with a note of take it or leave it.

"You take her no ware, I have built and repaired all your ships and no bloody government official is going to tell me what to do". He said quite firmly.

"I appreciate that". Mawgan replied as he held his hand out for the man to shake again, but thinking what's he up to.

"Now tell me before we get down to business, who is this beauty you have with you to-day".

Tamasine very lady like brought her leg over so she was sitting side saddle then slide down off the horse. "Tamasine Nancarrow". She said feeling quite charmed.

"Mawgan always kept his best possessions hid a way". The man said with a smile.

"Let me assure you sir I'm no one's possession". Tamasine replied as she held her hand out for the man to kiss.

"I think we should get down to business" Mawgan said trying to change the conversation and feeling a little jealous.

"Ok my friend what do you want us to do". The man asked as they all walked over to the ship.

"How many guns can you fit on her"? Mawgan asked as he pointed along the ship.

"Guns that's unlike you". The man said looking surprised.

"I have to go overseas for my work now, and we need to be well armed".

The man looked up and down the ship, putting his thumb up and looking over the top of it as if looking down the site of a musket. "She'll take thirty six cannon if its cannon you want". He replied.

"O its cannon I want". Mawgan replied. "How long before you have her ready".

"It'll take a couple of weeks, the man said where you going to take her?" he asked.

"Not sure yet" .Mawgan replied in a quiet voice.

"Well if you are going anywhere near Spain a load of ore would bring in a wealth of gold". The man whispered so that Tamasine couldn't hear.

"Exports are banded to France and Spain". Mawgan replied thinking what the hell is he up to.

"Exactly". The man replied.

Tamasine had been walking along the harbour a little way away from then, she had now returned. "We must go now". Mawgan said "Or we won't make Bodmin".

The man approached Tamasine and took her hand again and kissed it. "It's been a real pleasure to meet you and I hope you come again". He said with as large smile.

"The pleasure was all mine". Tamasine replied as she smiled back.

"Let me help you up on your horse". The man said as he bent down with his hands together for her to put her foot in.

"No need" Mawgan said as he got down in front of her doing the same.

"Why Mawgan I do believe your jealous". Tamasine said as the trotted out of the dock gate.

"What me jealous don't kid yourself". Mawgan replied as he gave Tamasine's horse a pat on the back.

"There is something about that man I don't trust". Tamasine said. "A bit too slimy for my likening".

"He's up to something no way he would have fitted out my ship else but at least it will get the job done". Mawgan and his horse were almost touching Tamasine and hers, even on horseback he wanted to get as close to her as he could.

They were about half an hour away from Bodmin when Mawgan said, "I think we should dismount and rest the horses a while".

They pulled up beside a stream that crossed the track they were on, they left the horses lose so they could drink from the stream and Mawgan and Tamasine sat on a grass bank beside the track.

Tamasine had a puzzled look on her face. "What you thinking" Mawgan asked sensing something was on her mind.

"You remember when Lilly Truman stole from Lord Giles".

"Yes".

"Well because she could not read or write and she stole to feed her family, she went in front of the clergy not a court".

"That's right they told her to work two days for Lord Giles to pay him back". Mawgan paused. "Why bring that up know". He asked.

"Because if she had the choice to go in front of the clergy why didn't Arthur, and Amy's mother. It's obvious she couldn't read". Tamasine thought the injustice just got bigger.

"Your right I think it's a question we should be asking, perhaps a visit to the court house first". Mawgan replied as he got up and got the horses together ready to mount up.

Mawgan helped Tamasine up on her horse and they were soon on their last bit of journey, they went straight to the court house, dismounted and walked up the four or five granite steeps to a large oak door, which

Mawgan banged on hard. It creaked as it opened and there standing in the door way was a short man with long grey shoulder length hair, "can I help you" he asked.

"We would like to know a few details about the case of Victoria Pringle if you don't mind". Mawgan said rather forcefully.

"What do you want to know"? The man paused, "She was hung you know". He replied in rather a sad voice.

"Yes we know, but was she offered to have her case heard by the clergy". Mawgan didn't think the man would answer.

The man shrugged his shoulders then beckoned them in side where they walked in to what can only be described as a ere court room. The man then picked up a card and handed to them, it was written with a quill it had the most beautiful writing and it explained people's rights. "She was given one of these". He said.

"She couldn't read". Tamasine replied furiously.

"That would have been for the judge to decide". The man replied.

Both Mawgan and Tamasine could tell that the man did not agree with what had happened. "Who was the judge". Mawgan asked.

"That would be Lord Tremeldon".

"Well we knew that didn't we!!" Tamasine said angrily.

"I know it was wrong I have to live with it, but what could I do, I have a family to feed, and Lord Tremeldon pays the wages around here". The man was almost in tears.

"Well if it was me I would have told her what rights she had, I would sooner starve then see someone hang". Tamasine thought the man a bit pathetic.

"In my book it is murder and I'm not sure it's legalised murder". Mawgan paused and rubbed his head. "Now could you tell us where Lord Tremeldon daughter lives"? He asked the man.

"She lives in the big house at Treant". The man replied. "You can't miss it t has two lions on the gate post's".

Mawgan and Tamasine left and it wasn't long before they were at Treant. In front of them were two large stone gateposts with a large lion carved on each of them. "This must be it". Mawgan said as they came to a halt beside the lions. They gingerly walked their horses up the long drive to the front door of the big house, they where meet by a smartly dressed man "can I help you" he asked.

"We would like to see the lady of the house". Mawgan said as the man took the reins of their horses.

"I will see if my lady is available". The man replied as he tied the horses on the other side of the drive from the house.

The man then entered the door, and it wasn't long before a well dressed woman of about thirty appeared. "Hello how can I help you"? She asked.

"Are you Lady Penrose?"Mawgan asked.

"I am Mrs Penrose". She replied. "But not a Lady I'm afraid". The women smiled.

"Let me introduce ourselves, this is Tamasine Nancarrow and I am Captain Mawgan".

"Pleased to meet you". The lady replied as she held her hand out for them both to shake.

"The reason for are visit is that Tamasine has two children living with her which are the children of the late Victoria Pringle". Before Mawgan finished what he was about to say the Lady interrupted him.

"My husband's children". She said in a sad voice. "You better come in".

She led them in to a large room and asked them to sit, she then called to the man they had meet when they arrived and asked him to bring tea for three to the drawing room.

"You know they are your husband's children"? Tamasine asked.

"Yes the poor things. I will never forgive my father for what he has done to that woman".

"You sound like you are concerned for them". Tamasine replied as she could see by the Lady's expression she was.

"I am I know Henry loved them and their mother we agreed he was going to leave me for them when he returned from America no matter what my father said".

"Did that trouble you". Mawgan asked.

"My goodness!! Not in the least I gave him my blessing, we should never have married, my heart was some ware else as was his".

"Then why!!" Tamasine asked". I don't understand.

"Both are parents pushed us in to it. Don't get me wrong I was fond of Henry we grew up together. Like brother and sister, but I never loved him in that way nor him me".

"I could never marry a man I didn't love". Tamasine said as she looked at Mawgan.

"I think if your Father was Lord Tremeldon you might think different I saw my lover whipped to an inch of his life".

"Why" Mawgan exclaimed.

"Because I wanted to be with him, Henry only married me to save my lovers life, that's the sort of man he was".

"We believe your father acted illegally when he had Victoria hung, she should have gone in front of the clergy not the court". Tamasine said sounding like some sort of lawyer.

"There is nothing legal that my Father does. But who's going to argue with him. The trouble is he is the law, he pays for the court and the officers".

Mawgan took the letter that they had found at Victories place out of his pocket and handed it to Mrs Penrose.

She slowly read it as if taking in every word, her eyes filling up with sadness. "It will take a while for my husband's affairs to be settled and when they are I will make sure they get what should be there's. My biggest regret is that I didn't go and see Victoria when my father told me my husband had died. I should have known better but just once I thought my father was showing some compassion when he said he would go and tell her. If only I knew what the bastard was up to." Mrs Penrose put a hanky to her eyes and whipped a tear before saying. "I'm so so sorry".

"We can give them love a home and guide them but it would be nice to think they had something in trust for when they are older". Tamasine put her arm around her to comfort her.

"I will make sure of that, do you think I could see them some time".

"Of course" Mawgan replied. "But what of you and your life".

"Me, I shall be going away with my real love as soon as Henry's estate is finalised, far away where my father will never find us".

"Good for you and if there is anything we can do just take the coach road from Penzance to Helston and you will find us". Mawgan reached over and shook the lady by the hand.

They bid there fair wells, and left with Mawgan and Tamasine thinking they had meet an incredible women.

It was dark when they got back home and called at Winnie's for the children, they were quite surprised to see James Wilmot Sparrow with Amy bouncing on his knee.

Chapter 10

After they had all gone home James told Winnie that he wanted to go out on the cliffs he said "it's time I started to watch by night".

"I'll come with you". Winnie replied she was sure nothing was going on around them that night.

James went to his bag and took out a telescope; the moon was shining as bright as day. He was convinced that if smuggling went on in the area it certainly would tonight.

Winnie picked up a towel and old blanket and put them under her arm. "What have you got those for"? James asked as he pulled his telescope in and out as if he was testing it.

"You don't think I'm going out on the cliffs with nothing to sit on do you". Winnie said as she opened the door and almost pushed James out.

They walked down the lane and out on to the edge of the cliff by Mawgan's cottage. Winnie laid out her blanket and they both sat down. Winnie laid right back and looked up at the stars. "Lilly-Rose say's all the information you ever need is in the stars". She said it as if Lilly-Rose said it, it must be right.

"Perhaps I should ask Lilly- Rose where the smugglers are". James replied as if he was teasing her.

"You may well laugh but there is nothing Lilly Rose doesn't know about anyone our anything". Winnie gently punched James on the arm as she said it.

"What does she say about me?" James asked still with a big smile on his face.

"I haven't asked her yet but believe me I will". Winnie replied with a big grin as she sat up beside James.

There where ships slowly sailing across the bay with little wind, the moon shining on their sales, lanterns glistening through the cabin windows.

"I don't believe I have seen a more beautiful site in my life". James said as he held his arms out wide as if to take it all in.

"I bet you have seen a few sites". Winnie replied knowing he had been watching her through the gap in the curtain at night.

"I have seen a few". He chuckled not realising that Winnie knew he had been watching her.

They sat there for more than an hour with James scouring the bay looking for unscrupulous goings on. "Come on". Winnie said as she stood up and picked up the towel, "let's go for a swim".

"Weee!! Can't". James stuttered. "We have nothing to wear".

"Don't worry about that there is only us two here". Winnie said as she bent down and caught hold of James's hand to pull him up.

"No, no I have to keep looking out to sea". James replied his face redder than Winnie's towel.

"Please yourself but I'm going you don't know what you might be missing". Winnie made her way down to the beach.

"I won't miss a thing". James said to himself as he taped his telescope on his hand.

Winnie was on the beach she put her towel on the rock, and slowly removed her cloths she didn't once look up towards James but she knew he had his telescope peeled on her; she undressed in such a teasing way that she was naked yet showed nothing.

Winnie swam for about twenty minutes before she came in and dried herself keeping her back to James then turning gently to one side, in the same teasing way as she did when she got undressed. She made her way up the cliff back to where James was sitting. "Have you seen anything of interest"? She asked.

"Plenty of interest". James said to himself, then a. "No". To Winnie.

"What shall we do now"? Winnie asked.

"I would like to walk down around the harbour it looks quite beautiful in moonlight". James said as he rolled the blanket up that they had been sitting on.

"Are you getting all romantic or do you just want to go and see Lowenna". Winnie laughed.

"I want to go no ware near that woman". He replied quite forcefully.

They walked down around the harbour and back to Winnie's cottage; all the way Winnie was tempted to slip her hand in to James's, but worried how he would react. She was beginning to get quite fond of him.

The following morning when Tamasine and the children arrived at Mawgan's he was sat at a large wooden table in the garden he had nautical charts laid out in front of him. "What you up to"? Tamasine asked as she came over and put her arm around his shoulder.

"Planning my trip". Came an enthusiastic reply.

"I wish you wouldn't go it is so dangerous". Tamasine removed her arm and picked up Arthur and put him on the hammock and started to push him to and fro.

"You sound like you would miss me". Mawgan stood up and picked up Amy and placed her on the hammock with Arthur.

"Don't kid yourself it's your safety I'm worried about". Tamasine smiled.

"If my plan works the only danger will come from the sea". Mawgan smiled back.

"And what plan is that may I ask"? Tamasine wanted to be involved.

"All in good time". Mawgan replied as Willy and Rajah appeared.

They both said there good mornings. Willy went right over and picked Amy up off the hammock and swung her around. Arthur was moving himself back and forward to make the hammock go higher. It was like some of the grown up mannerisms he had when he arrived had gone. The natural child had come out in him, and this pleased Tamasine.

"Willy!!" Mawgan exclaimed "I need a crew of thirty six good men, men that would fight if necessary". All Mawgan's ships crews had left, many had found other ships sailing out of Penzance or Falmouth some had returned to the mines.

"You have two here *Cap'n*". Willy said. "Me and Rajah".

"No I need you two here, to look after my affairs, O and my women". Mawgan smiled and put his arm around Tamasine and pulled her tight to him.

"I'm nobody's women". Tamasine pulled herself away.

"Talking of women I need to catch Winnie on her own". Mawgan smiled as he knew what the response would be.

Tamasine looked angrily at him. "You just can't leave her alone can you".

"Well you said it your nobody's women, well I'm nobody's man, but if you are concerned you can come with me when I go to see her". Mawgan new she was jealous.

"May I suggest we all have a cup of tea." Rajah said as he could see Tamasine was getting annoyed.

"What a good Idea" .Mawgan replied.

Rajah went into the kitchen and soon returned with a large pot of tea and cups with a jug of milk all on a tray. He placed the tray on the table set out the cups and preceded to poor. The gate opened and Winnie and James entered, James immediately thought he was on to something. "Is that tea I see"?

"Would you like a cup?" Rajah paused knowing it was smuggled. "Ah is that all right Captain. Rajah knows it is very expensive".

"We spare no expense on our distinguished guests". Mawgan walked over beside James. "How are your investigations going on?"

"I have seen no sign of any smuggling; this is the first tea I have seen come to that". James would still like to know where it came from.

"Yes not many folk can afford it I bought a little in Bodmin as a treat for my friends". Mawgan picked up the cup that Rajah had poured and handed it to James.

"It has to be so deer to pay for our wars". James stood almost to attention as he said it.

"Not our wars, I see no point in wars". Mawgan said as he looked out to sea.

"We have many colonies around the world, we discovered them we own them, we rule them, now we educate them and they want to rule them self's". James stood like he was preaching a sermon.

"Let them rule there self's let's just stand back and say what a good job we done by educating them". Mawgan paused then he returned to where James was standing he then continued. "A women was hung because she stole to feed her children, they tell me London streets are full of hungry children, we have people working down our mines for a penny an hour to try and feed their kids, you want to spend some tea money spend it on them I say".

James could see Mawgan was angry. "We just can't let savages rule there self's". He replied feeling just a little embarrassed.

"Come on let's not fall out about it". Winnie said trying to calm the situation.

"I 'm not going to fall out, I just want James to understand if he did happen to find some smugglers, which I very much doubt, they aren't criminals they are just people trying to feed their families". Mawgan put his hand out for James to shake.

James shook his hand and never let ago until he finished saying. "I don't know the answers but there has to be laws. Like it or not they are made by our government and we have solders out in America fighting and without weapons, they will be slaughtered".

"We will just have to disagree on some things". Mawgan said. "Now how about another tea.

"No thank you I have to catch the ten o'clock coach to Truro then the coach to Plymouth, I have to report to my employers in the morning".

"What have you to report?" Tamasine asked.

"Nothing absolutely nothing".

"Will you be retuning?"Mawgan asked if he didn't one of his plans would have gone for a burden.

"Yes in couple of days the message I received say's they have a position for me in Penzance".

"Will you stay at Winnie's when you come back?" Tamasine asked hoping he would as there was no chance for Mawgan to call when James was staying.

"Of course". Winnie answered before James had a chance to say a word.

James left to catch the coach Winnie left to see him off, Tamasine and the children stayed at Mawgan's most of the day in between going down on the beach and paddling. Willy was trying to persuade Mawgan to give him six pence to spend at Lowenna's. "That would be the best place to recruit a crew". He told Mawgan.

"You might be right". Mawgan replied as he took six pence out of his pocket and tossed to him. "What about you Rajah do you want six pence". Mawgan took another few coins from his pocket.

"I would very much like six pence but I save mine". Rajah replied with a look of gratitude.

"sixpence *in ardly* enough to save". Willy replied full of excitement to where he was going.

"Six pence here and a penny there you would be surprised how it grows". Rajah was really grateful for what Mawgan had given him.

"*Tis* surprising *ow e* grows!! When *E* spends it down Lowenna's". Willy replied with a large grin.

It was almost seven o clock when Tamasine left to put the children to bed, and Willy had gone to Lowenna's, Rajah had gone for a walk along the cliff, Mawgan had decided to go and see Winnie.

Winnie was sitting in the garden when Mawgan got there. "Would you like a drink"? Was the greeting he got when entered the garden.

"Elderberry cordial would be fine". He replied.

Winnie went in and soon returned with two beakers of cordial, she passed one to Mawgan and then sat down beside him. "It's nice of you to call I have missed you coming around." She said then took a sip of her drink.

"How much have me have you missed". Mawgan rested his hand on her knee.

"I have missed everything that you do". Winnie lifted his hand off her knee.

"Is there something wrong?" Mawgan asked sensing Winnie's unease.

"O my mind is not on it, god I want you, you know how to please me; but its pleasure not love" .Winnie stood up and turned her back on Mawgan.

Mawgan stood up and gently kissed her on the back of the neck. "What's wrong with a little pleasure"? He asked.

"Pleasure is what people like Lowenna give, I want more". Winnie said as she turned and looked Mawgan in the eye.

"I can't give you love as you want it". Mawgan replied.

"I know and I can't love you in that way, beside's we all know where your heart is". Winnie stretched up and kissed him on the cheek.

Mawgan smiled at her. "I better tell you why I'm here then". He then sat down on the seat.

"You mean you didn't come here for my body after all". Winnie replied trying to sound disappointed.

"I did have that on my mind, but I do have another motive".

"And what might that be"? Winnie asked with a smile.

 I wondered if you have seen the letter James had from the King".

"I have why".

"Do you think it genuine?"

"I have no reason to think otherwise he is very proud of it". Winnie frowned.

"When he comes back do you think you could sneak it out for me to borrow, I would only need it for a couple of hours?" Mawgan was sounding persuading.

"O I don't know why do you want it".

"Please don't ask just trust me."

"He hasn't taken it with him" .Winnie was a bit concerned but new Mawgan could be trusted and if he wanted it must be for a good reason.

"That's even better I could borrow it now and you could put it back tomorrow" Mawgan gave her a kiss on the cheek as if to say it will be all right.

"I am not sure it is right to go through his things when he is not here, but I trust you and know it must be important". Winnie got up and went in to his bedroom and returned with the letter it was easy to find as he slept with it beside his bed.

Mawgan took the letter and kissed her good night, "I will tell you one day what it's for it might save a lot of lives". Mawgan left felling rather pleased.

Chapter 11

The next morning Mawgan went down on the beach and walked along looking for an old friend and artist who arrived on the shores many years ago from France, he went by the name of Henri. Henri lived in a small wooden shack at the far end of the beach which doubled as a studio. Henri lived on a diet of smoked fish and rum, the latter supplied by Mawgan.

Henri was sitting outside his shack on a rock smoking a clay pipe his face was black what you could see of it underneath a large curly tangled beard that matched his hair you couldn't see were the beard finished and the hair began. "Mawgan my friend" he shouted as Mawgan approached.

"Henri!!" Mawgan shouted in reply.

"Mawgan my friend you seem to be empty handed". Henri said expecting to see a flagon of rum in his hand.

"First things first if you can do something for me I will bring you barrels not flagons". Mawgan replied quite calmly.

"You better come and sit beside me my friend". Henri pated the rock beside him.

Mawgan sat down on the rock beside him, trying not to breath in to sharply as Henri smelt of a mixture of fish tobacco and rum, the three of them together was not at all pleasant. Mawgan produced the king's letter out of his pocket. "Tell me my friend you are good with a quill are you not".

"The best no one writes like Henri"

"If I tell you what to write can you copy that writing?"Mawgan asked.

"Treason my friend that's Treason". Henri replied as he handed the letter back to Mawgan.

"I don't think it's quite Treason". Mawgan was trying to make light of the matter.

"Not for me as I am a Frenchman, it's an act of war and I would be shot but for you my friend its treason and you would be hung".

"No matter can you do it?"

Henri stood up. "Come" he said as he made his way in to his shack.

Mawgan followed as they entered the shack Mawgan's jaw dropped as he looked at a large painting on an easel by the window. The painting was quite large it must have been all of three foot square.

"You like". Henri asked knowing too well he would.

"It's beautiful". Mawgan replied softly.

The painting was of Tamasine she was naked sitting by a rock on the beach, she was topless and Henri had painted a mermaids bottom half. "I think she is the most beautiful women I have ever painted". Henri picked up a quill and a piece of paper his hand was shaking, which stopped as soon as he dipped the quill into some ink and wrote some letters on the paper. "How does that look"? He asked as he handed the paper to Mawgan, who had not taken his eyes of the painting.

"That's fine; now tell me did she pose for you". Mawgan asked as his eyes went straight back on to the painting.

"No I watched her every morning when she came down to bathe. I held every feature every line and mark in my mind; I could paint her again now without seeing her".

"I want to buy it" Mawgan gasped.

"It's not for sale my friend" Henri said as he took the piece of paper he had written the letters on from Mawgan.

"Everything is for sale at a price so name yours". Mawgan really wanted this Painting.

"My friend when money means nothing to you everything is not for sale. Now tell me my friend what do you want this letter to say"

"You disappoint me as you won't sale me the painting. As for the letter it needs to read to a captain as if an order from the king to collect Annabel the daughter of the Earl of West Moorland". Mawgan suddenly went deep in thought.

"What name has this Captain" Henri asked.

"Captain Walter Dark of the Kings special force's, how does that sound?" Mawgan replied.

"It sounds good to me, if you return to night I will have it done, complete with royal seal".

"I look forward to it" Mawgan reached out and shook Henri's hand.

Mawgan turned and started to go out of the door of the shack when Henri shouted, "you have forgotten something".

"What?" Mawgan asked as he turned to Face Henri.

"Your picture my friend, your picture", Henri handed Mawgan the painting.

"But you said it's not for sale".

"Nor is it my friend it's a gift from a foolish French man to an even more foolish English man".

"I really appreciate it but how do you mean foolish". Mawgan asked as he took the painting from Henri.

"To do what you are planning is more than foolish, but I wish you luck I think you will need it". Henri taped Mawgan on the shoulder.

Mawgan just smiled. "Right is on my side". He said as he left Henri and made his way back to his cottage with the painting he kept holding it up in front of him admiring every bit of it.

He hadn't been back long when Tamasine and the two children arrived. "What's that you are holding" she asked as Mawgan was stood admiring his painting.

"O nothing" he replied putting the painting down with the front towards the wall.

"Let's have a look then" Tamasine went towards the painting.

"O you wouldn't like it; it's just some old thing Henri let me have". Mawgan stood between her and the painting.

"I like his paintings"

"Not this one you wouldn't". Mawgan was determined she wouldn't see it yet.

70

But Tamasine was even more determined she would. "I don't see how an old painting can make you so nervous". She said as she pushed past Mawgan and lifted it up. "My God it's me".

"Isn't it beautiful" Mawgan gasped.

"I'm not so sure about that, did Henri paint it?" Tamasine blushed.

"Yes he gave it to me this morning".

"Has he been watching me naked on the beach?"

"I would think so; he seems to have your body just right". Mawgan smiled at her.

"How do you know? Have you been watching me as well?" Tamasine had wanted Mawgan to see her as she was teasing him, but was rather embarrassed that someone else had seen her also.

"How could any man keep his eyes off a mermaid like you?"Mawgan put his arm around her.

"I liked being naked on the beach and swimming that way, but now I shall never be able to do it again". Tamasine sulked.

"You can always be naked in my bed". Mawgan smiled.

"You can dream of that like you dream of mermaids". Tamasine said as she turned and picked Amy up.

"Why don't you take the children down on the beach I have to go up to Winnie's, I will join you when I return". Mawgan picked up Arthur "what do you think of that little man". He said as he lifted him high above his head.

"I suppose you think you will catch Winnie in her bed". Tamasine said quite angrily.

"No chance of that I think are Winnie is in love". Mawgan replied with a smile.

"What with James Wilmot thing E". Tamasine frowned.

"It would seem so".

Mawgan left and Tamasine and the children started to make their way down to the beach. They had only just got there when they were approached by the man she had met at Falmouth docks with Mawgan. "A pleasure to meet such a thing of beauty again" the man said.

"O hello are you looking for Mawgan". Tamasine asked quite startled.

"I do have business with him, but I would like to spend some time with you". The man put his hand on her shoulder.

Tamasine turned quickly so that the man's hand dropped off. "I have things to do". She replied as she bent down and picked up Amy and started to walk across the beach.

"Please tell me I haven't upset you". The man said in a soft voice.

"You haven't upset me Sir but I do have to attend the children". Tamasine hoping this would get rid of him.

"I can help you with them". He replied.

"I'd rather you went and attended to your business with Mawgan". Tamasine replied quite forcefully.

Mawgan had returned and made his way down to the beach, and went over to greet the man. "How's my ship" he asked.

"Should be ready next week". The man replied.

Mawgan led the man back up too his cottage "I suppose you have come to collect payment". He said as they reached the cottage door.

"That would be nice, but my main reason is have you thought any more about what I said regarding taking some ore to Spain".

"I have thought about it, but I don't think anyone will sell ore to me". Mawgan opened the door and they went inside.

"You will have to find a way to take it then". The man said as he sat down.

"I won't steal". Mawgan said forcefully.

"You're too good Mawgan, how much money do they owe you?"

"I will still not steal a little bit of duty is one thing but I am an honest man". Mawgan sighed.

"I know that Mawgan but just think this is the only way you will be paid". The man was getting quite persuasive.

After a lot of chat Mawgan finally agreed that he would take seventy ton and no more just to cover what he was owed. He new deep down he was being set up but he was convinced he could out smart him.

The man left saying he would send a message when his ship was ready.

Mawgan walked back down to the beach where Tamasine and the children were playing. "I don't trust that man" Tamasine said as Mawgan approached.

"I thought you found him quite a charmer" Mawgan laughed.

"The charm I can deal with it's the slime I can't". Tamasine said with some conviction.

Chapter 12

The following day James Wilmot Sparrow returned with news of his new job in Penzance. He came down to Mawgan's were he found Winnie and Mawgan with Tamasine and the children. "What is this mystery job you have?"Mawgan asked with a little chuckle.

"I am to be in charge of the customs house in Penzance" James replied with a tone of excitement.

Mawgan looked concerned. "Tell me James Wilmot Sparrow do you own a pistol" he asked.

"Why" James frond.

"Because no one lives for more than a few months in that job". Mawgan replied.

"Mawgan is that true" Winnie asked "or are you teasing".

"I wouldn't tease about that". Mawgan turned to James, "I hope you will reconsider that job is not safe for any man".

"I serve my King and country and I do not fear this job I always have right on my side". James replied in a determined tone.

"Right!! Do you think our King knows right"? This was one of Mawgan's passions. "Children starving, women hung for trying to feed them. Don't talk to me about right". Mawgan said quite angrily.

Winnie put her arms around James. "It's not James's fault he is only doing a job he believes in". She said softly.

"There has to be rules" James said "or else there would be anakey".

"What do you think we have now, who decides who keeps to the rules, who pays you, I bet it's not the king or his government". Mawgan certainly made his feelings known.

Winnie was getting quite upset, "Of course the government pay him".

"No they don't I get paid by a group of people in Plymouth and Cornwall".

"Who are these people?" Winnie asked.

"I don't know all of them but they are made up of Earl's lords and businessmen". James took a deep breath then continued, "Good honest god faring people, people that have our King and country at heart".

Tamasine picked Amy up "James you're a nice guy and I hope you come to no harm but I'm with Mawgan on this".

"Look I have only known you all for a short time but I will do my job, a job I believe in, if children are starving perhaps you are looking in the wrong place, it's the owners of the mines, and factory's the people that pay them that are at fault". James said.

"That's right". Mawgan replied. "The same people that pay you".

The arguments and discussions went on for quite some time before James and Winnie went back to Winnie's cottage.

Tamasine put her arm around Mawgan, "I don't want you in Winnie's bed but I hope you haven't lost her as a friend". She said as she held him tight.

"O she will never desert me as a friend, as for the bed there is only one person I want in my bed". Mawgan replied as he bent forward and kissed her on the forehead.

Tamasine looked up and smiled, and then broke away. "I have to play with the kids".

Mawgan still had one of his ships tied up on his Quay. He had heard that they were going to load two ships with ore over at Long Quay which was the other side of the cliff from his Quay.

Mawgan shouted for Willy "What *E* want *Cap'n*". Willy replied as he came running towards him.

"An early start for you tomorrow". Mawgan had as smile all over his face.

"Doing what *Cap'n*". Willy had a puzzled look on his face.

"I need you to get the horse early in the morning and hitch up the cart. They are loading ore at Long Quay from Shallow Grave Mine". Mawgan had a look of mischief on his face.

"You want us to help *um Cap'n*". Willy was sounding surprised.

"No we are going to help our self's".

"*Ow's* us going to do that?"

"You join the queue for loading at the mine when they go to Long Quay you come down to ours and tip, then wait up the top of the track and join the queue in the same place, you do this for two days until we have fifty ton". Mawgan had a smug look about him.

"Will us get away with it?"Willy was a little concerned.

"We will if you go in the same place in the queue each time". Mawgan taped Willy on the shoulder.

"You *kin* count on me I'll go check the cart *drekly*, I might give the *oses* a bit more *ay*". Willy was now very excited.

Winnie left James up at her cottage and walked down to the quay where Lilly- Rose was sitting, clay pipe in the corner of her mouth. "You look troubled Winnie Triwin". She said as Winnie approached.

"O' Lilly I'm so confused over right and wrong". Winnie said in a disenchanted way as she sat down beside her.

Lilly taped her on the leg and laughed, which came deep from a throat that had more bac-ey down it over the years than food. "What some people say is right may be wrong, and what some people say is wrong may be right".

"That confuses things more than ever I just don't understand" .Winnie frowned.

"The man you love believes he is doing right for King and country, and that's all that matters he is doing what he believes is right". Lilly taped her leg again trying to reassure her.

"I'm not in love with James he is just staying with me". Winnie looked quite embarrassed.

"Aren't you dear then why the concern".

"I consider him as a friend, but his differences with Mawgan worry me, I owe Mawgan so much". Winnie sighed.

"Don't worry about Mawgan he will always be a friend to you, and all of us no matter what". Lilly new Mawgan better than anyone.

"I do hope so". Winnie left and made her way back to her cottage and James.

The following morning Willy left with the horse and cart at around five AM. It was around the same time that James left to walk to Penzance to take up his new position. Willy arrived at Shallow Grave Mine sixth in the queue for loading; he could not have planed it better. In no time the carts where loaded by about thirty men. Some who new Willy looked surprised to see him but said nothing. Willy just kept enough distance from the cart in front so that he would not be noticed when he turned off. Willy turned down towards the quay as planed tipped his load then returned to the top of the track waited for the cart he followed from the mine to return and then followed it back for another load. This continued all day.

Mean while over in Penzance James was finding what a difficult task he had. His main task was to recruit some helpers who would be paid twenty five pounds for every smuggler caught and sixpence for every item of contraband seized. This was so much money James thought he would have a dozen men by the end of the day. But all he got was a load of abuse, he was spat on punched kicked and even had the odd chamber pot or two thrown over him. He returned home to Winnie's that night tired and rejected but determined he would do his job smuggling would be controlled.

As James reached the cottage gate Winnie was there to meet him she could see he was in some distress. "Whatever has happened to you" she asked as she looked at his eyes that were both black.

"Savages animals!! That's the only way I can describe those people". He replied.

"Come on in you poor thing, you must have a bath you are smelling and your poor eyes, whatever have they done to you". Winnie put her arm around him and led him in doors.

Winnie went out the back and dragged the large tin bath over in front of the fire she took two large kettles of water of the fire and poured them in the bath. She had the water ready as she thought James would want a bath but did not expect him in this state. "Aren't you going to get in then?"Winnie asked as she tested the temperature of the water with her hand.

"I will when you have gone" .He stuttered.

"I forgot you were a shy boy". Winnie had such a teasing way about her. She got up gave James a kiss on the cheek. "I'll see you later". Winnie smiled and went out the door. She ran down too Mawgan's who sat at a table with maps and charts in front of him. "I suppose your happy now". Winnie shouted as she entered the cottage.

"How do you mean". Mawgan replied with a surprised look on his face.

"James". She shouted.

"James what about James"? Mawgan was still none the wiser.

"He has been punched kicked had stuff thrown over him". Winnie was really angry.

"I'm sorry about that but I did try to warn him". Mawgan put his arm around her.

"It's not fair he is only trying to do what he thinks is right". Winnie started to cry.

"Hay you really do love him don't you". Mawgan smiled at her.

"I'm just concerned someone might kill him, can't you talk to the people they will listen to you". Winnie pleaded.

"People just can't change their way of life, if James wants to do his job he will have to do it slowly, and turn a blind eye to a lot of things". Mawgan stressed.

"I don't think he will do that". Winnie wiped her tears.

"Then I'm sorry there is nothing I can do". Mawgan took the hanky from Winnie and dried her eyes in a caring way.

Winnie returned to her cottage where James had had his bath, Winnie dragged the bath outside and tipped the water away. "I have a nice piece of Willy's bacon for tea". She said as she refilled the kettles and put them on the fire.

James eat his tea as if he hadn't eaten for months, the day had certainly taken it out of him, it wasn't long before James was asleep in the chair, Winnie quietly dragged the bath in and tipped the kettles of water in. She was just beginning to get undressed when James woke up. "O I'm sorry I'll go out". He said as he started to get up from the chair.

Winnie put her finger up to her lips. "Shh!! no need you just rest".

James lay back in the chair he could not take his eyes off her as she slowly undone the buttons on her dress and let it drop to the ground. The room was dark except for the light of the fire and a small lantern hanging from the ceiling, her naked body looked bronze and glowing in the dim light. Beautiful he whispered to himself.

Winnie got in to the bath and soaped herself all over she could see James could not take his eyes of her. "Would you like to wash my back?" She asked quietly in a way no man would have resisted.

James never uttered a word he just nervously nodded, as Winnie past him a sponge. James gently ran the sponge down over her back his hands shaking like autumn leaves on a beech tree. James spent a couple of minutes running the sponge up and down. "Why don't you try it without the sponge?" Winnie whispered.

James dropped the sponge and gently caressed her up and down her back. Winnie took his hand and gently brought it around her front and placed it on her breast why don't you try this side". She whispered.

James gently caressed her breast his face getting close to Winnie's , it wasn't long before their lips touched James kissed her with such passion you would never have known it was his first kiss.

"I have to get out now". Winnie whispered.

She stood up and James handed her a towel. "You going to dry me". She asked teasingly.

James gently dried every part of her body, when she was dry she took the towel from James through it on the floor caught hold of his hand and led him to her bed. "It's my turn". Now she said as she started to undo his shirt. It wasn't long before James was completely naked and flopped on Winnie's bed. They spent the whole night in Winnie's bed.

Chapter 13

Things had all gone well with Willy he had the fifty tons of ore loaded on Mawgan's ship that was tied up at the quay. James was still getting a hard time from the folk in Penzance so much so that some men from Plymouth had been sent down to help him, one being an ugly brut who went under the name of Slaughter House he would break a man's neck for tupence .

It was late in the afternoon when the man from Falmouth had called to say Mawgan's ship had been fitted out and was ready for collection; Tamasine was again down at Mawgan's when the man arrived. The man again made a bee line for her, telling her what a thing of beauty she was, in a way that Tamasine found quite sickening. She was quite pleased when Mawgan took him to one side. "I believe we have business to discuss". Mawgan said leading the man to the garden.

"Were you going to sail your ship to, now she's all fitted out with cannon"? The man asked "Spain with a cargo of ore I hope".

The man was Albert Stoneham the son of Sir Fredrik Stoneham Mawgan knew he was close to Lord Tremeldon but he didn't know close. Sir Fredrik and Lord Tremeldon's businesses where entangled, that's how Mawgan knew he was being set up.

"I'm going to take a load of ore to Spain as you suggested that's if you pay me, and then who knows". Mawgan pulled a chair out in the garden for the man to sit down.

"Very wise when do you think you will get the ore, I can let my contact no to expect you with delivery".

"Don't worry about the ore I can sort that, what about payment". If Mawgan was being set up he was going to make sure he would have the last laugh.

"My man will pay you when you arrive in Spain".

"No deal then, I want the money before I sail, in fact I want the money from you .How else can I be sure of payment". Mawgan thought he could

80

keep the money for the children after all it was money that lord Tremeldon owed them, and he was sure he was behind the set up.

"How can I be sure you will carry it through?" The man obviously was feeling uneasy.

"One thing for sure I know you can trust me to deliver the ore, but something tells me I can't trust you". Mawgan stood up as if there business had finished.

"Now wait a minute I will pay you when you pick your ship up, now when are you sailing out". There was a look on the man's face like he had just rescued a situation.

I will collect the ship on Monday sail her around here load her and set sail on Fridays tied.

The man put his hand out for Mawgan to shake, his hand was limp a hand shake that Mawgan thought meant nothing. The man then mounted his horse and left.

"He gives me the creeps". Tamasine said as she came out to the garden with the children.

"I'm pretty sure I know what he's up to, and I know why he worked on my ship when no one else would". Mawgan put his arm around Tamasine. "Will you miss me when I'm gone. "He asked quietly.

"You know I will, so will all of us. Tell me what's that man called beside's creep". She laughed.

"Albert Stoneham his father is Sir Frederic Stoneham, he owns most of the docks from here to Plymouth he is also big on law and order, along with other business, they pay people to try and keep the law".

"Is that like James dose?"Tamasine was intrigued.

"I would think that's who James works for him Lord Tremeldon and a few Plymouth business men". Mawgan rubbed his chin "I don't know of another organisation like it".

"Gosh!! So what is he trying to do with you"? Tamasine was fearful for Mawgan.

"I think he wants me arrested he is trying to encourage me to break the law, I just hope I'm smarter than him".

Tamasine leaned up and gave Mawgan a kiss. "Smarter than him in every way. But promise me whatever you are up too you will be careful".

"I do believe you care about me". Mawgan laughed.

"I care about you more than you will ever know". Tamasine replied with a very sad face.

"If you really cared you would share my bed before I go". Mawgan put his arm around her and squeezed her tight.

Tamasine put her arm around him and cuddled in close. "Please Mawgan don't ask me like this, I am so worried for you, I just don't want to give in to your wishes like this. If ever I do it's because I want it to be for the right reasons. I want it to mean something to you; I want it to be for life". Tamasine was sounding so serious.

Mawgan pushed her back; he put a hand on each shoulder and looked her in the eye. "It would mean something, in fact it would mean everything to me, but I won't ask you again until I return from my voyage".

"Thank you". Tamasine leaned up and kissed Mawgan again. "Now I'm going to take the children down to the harbour for a while". Tamasine spoke as if a weight had been lifted from her shoulders.

After Tamasine had left, Mawgan called for Willy, who always came running as soon as called. Rajah also appeared down the chimney he was working on the hiding place which was a deep cave behind the fire place, but now they had fixed the fire place firmly to the ground and wall, and you entered the cave buy climbing up the inside of the chimney. "You called *Cap'n*". Willy asked standing up straight in front of Mawgan.

"Yes!! Where can I find Captain Pendray"? He was a Captain that sailed one of Mawgan's ships.

"He has been known to visit Lowenna's a few nights a week". Willy was excited hoping it would be him that would have to fetch him.

"I will have to see if he is there tonight". Mawgan replied knowing what would come next from Willy.

"I could see *im* if you like, only I got no money". Willy looked at Mawgan like a dog pleading for a bone.

82

Mawgan took six pence out of his waist coat pocket and tossed it to him. "Whilst you are there I want you to tell all the sailors that are heading out about a fierce red haired captain that the King has. He is a man of iron, with a tough fighting force that no man would argue with, he has hair and a beard so red that the like has never been seen before, they say he can kill a man with his little finger". Mawgan had Willy mesmerised.

"A*ve* you met this *Cap'n*"? Willy asked with fear in his eyes.

"O yes I have met him he is Captain Walter Dark a man everyone should fear and tomorrow you can go to Penzance and tell everyone there".

"I'll spread the word *Cap'n* you can rely on me".

"Yes I believe I can". Mawgan laughed.

Tamasine had taken the children down to the harbour; every time she went down she couldn't resist spending some time with Lilly-Rose". You look pleased with yourself". Lilly-Rose said as Tamasine and the children appeared, a smile appeared through a face full of wrinkles as she said "you look like a girl in love".

"O Lilly!! I don't think I know how to love". Tamasine sighed.

"It's the most natural thing in the world everyone knows how to give love when the time is right. Let me see its Mawgan isn't it". Lilly pretended she had just worked it out but of course she knew who it was.

"Am I being selfish not giving in to him, I'm sure I love him, sometimes he makes my body ache my hart pounds like Joseph the blacksmith's bellows, so much so it's hard to bear, I feel I should just say take me now". Tamasine sighed. "I just don't want to share him I want him to myself, tell me Lilly is that being selfish". She asked.

"No dear! Girls like Lowenna are for sharing, girls like you are for loving, Mawgan will see that don't worry, all men think they can have it both ways for awhile you mark my words, Mawgan will want to settle soon". Lilly gently caught hold of her hand.

"I hope it's soon I do fear so for him". Tamasine rested her hand across Lilly's.

Tamasine left Lilly and played with the children down on the quay for a while before returning to her cottage.

That night Willy went and visited Lowenna's and when he left everyone was talking about Captain Walter Dark.

Captain Pendray had gone up to see Mawgan who asked him if he would sail the ship in the harbour to Spain Pendray agreed.

Mawgan wanted him to sail the ship to Spain then he would leave two days later with the ship that has had the guns fitted and he would pick Pendray and crew up from Spain, as he planned to sell the ship there as well as the ore. Then both crews would go on to India so he wanted to sail both ships with a limited crew. It was decided that they would both sail with a crew of fifteen, and they would meet on Sunday to finalise the plans.

Chapter 14

Sunday came around and Captain Pendray came to Mawgan's where they were to discuss the final arrangements for their trips. Pendray told how he had sorted both crews but had not told them what their trip entailed nor were they were going. Both crews would be down on the quay on Wednesday.

Willy came in as the discussions were going on. "Can I come with *E* Cap'n"? He asked.

"No Willy I told you I need you to stay here to look after the place I will ask Tamasine to stay here in the cottage, then you can look after her and the children. Make sure Rajah still stays hidden when strangers are around". Willy now felt important.

"How long will *E* be away *Cap'n?*" Willy wanted to know how long he would be important for.

"Six months or quicker with good winds, but don't worry I will leave you a sixpence or two so that you can visit Lowenna" .Mawgan chuckled.

"*Thank-e Cap'n*". Willy replied wondering how many sixpences there would be.

Pendray said he would go to Falmouth the next morning with Mawgan to bring his ship around to the quay. Mawgan said he was going to take Tamasine and the children with them so that they could have trip on the ship, they would get Willy to take them there with the horse and trap. Mawgan and Pendray shook hands and agreed to meet at six the next morning to go to Falmouth.

The next morning Amy and Arthur where all excited about their trip, Willy had the horse and trap all ready by five thirty and by six they were on their way. As they were making their way there Pendray asked Mawgan. "Do you know who in Spain will buy the ship and contents"?

"I hope a very old friend of my father's is still at Santandare he had a lot of contacts and he always paid in gold. He always stayed with us when he was over on business I think it was dodgy business but my father never told me". Mawgan was just a little apprehensive.

"What if he's not there?"Pendray thought Mawgan was leaving it a bit to chance.

"Then we will just have to trust to luck". Mawgan replied.

Although the journey took nearly two hours to get to Falmouth it seemed no time at all as the children hadn't stopped chatting all the way.

They where meet by Albert Stoneham he first went to Tamasine, "I see you have difficulty in keeping away from me". He said.

"In your dreams". She whispered in reply.

"O my dear I do dream about you every night, I dream you will be mine one day". Albert had such a slimy smile.

"I think we should talk business". Mawgan said leading Albert away from Tamasine.

"Not jealous are you Mawgan". Albert said as turned back to look at Tamasine as Mawgan led him in to his office.

They got in to the Office an Albert sat at his desk. "I have done you a bill of sale for the work to your ship". He said still trying to look out of the window at Tamasine.

Mawgan pulled a bankers note out of his pocket. "Here is a promise of payment from my bank". He replied passing the note to Albert.

Albert looked at it for a moment or two. "That seems fine".

"Now!!" Mawgan said quite forcefully. "What about payment for the ore".

Albert took a small bag which was tied at the top out from under his desk, "gold you asked for wasn't it". Albert pushed the bag over to Mawgan but keeping on hand on top of it. "Now how do I know you will keep to your end of the bargain?"Albert had his hand tightly on the bag.

"If you don't trust me best I leave now". Mawgan started to stand up.

"My dear Mawgan of course I trust you". Albert took his hand of the bag for Mawgan to pick up, which he did and put it in his pocket. "Aren't you going to cheek it?"

"I think I can trust you". Mawgan replied knowing quite well he couldn't.

"Let me take you to your ship now". Albert said as he got up from his chair.

They made their way down to the ship the others had already gone down there and were aboard. It wasn't long before Mawgan joined them and they had a sail hoisted, "when are you sailing for Spain"? Albert shouted.

"Friday's high tied". Came the reply.

Pendray looked at Mawgan, "I thought we were sailing out on Wednesday". He said.

"You are" Mawgan replied.

"And you". Pendray asked.

"I sail on Friday, hears the plan you sail the ship that's back at the quay loaded with ore anchor just of the port of Spain, I will sail on Friday when I think there could be a little trouble, but what every happens I will meet you at the port of Spain". Mawgan pulled a piece of paper out of his pocket. "This is the name of my father's friend in Spain. Like 1 said before, I don't know if he still lives, but he had children so someone will know someone who will buy". Mawgan had the look of excitement about him.

"Shall I sail in to port before you arrive?" Pendray asked.

"I think that for the best after all we aren't at war at the moment". Mawgan replied as he pulled on the rope of the main sale.

The wind was strong and by late afternoon they were back at Mawgan's Quay. Pendray left and said he would return on Wednesday with his crew, he would also bring Mawgan's crew they could sleep on the ship until they sailed.

Tamasine, Mawgan and the children were walking up from the quay; the children ran on up to Lilly-Rose as soon as they saw her sitting outside her cottage smoking her clay pipe. "Come here my dears". Lilly shouted as soon as she saw them.

The children ran and sat beside her it wasn't long before they were joined by Mawgan and Tamasine who also sat down. "You all ready for your trip Mawgan"? Lilly asked.

"I shall sale further than I have ever sailed before". Mawgan replied with a note of boyhood excitement.

"You never sailed further than the Long rocks before, you *could-en* pass the mermaids they say". Lilly laughed.

"Why Mawgan it's the first time I have seen you embarrassed". Tamasine also laughed.

"Is there really mermaids?" Arthur asked.

"Plenty of men say they have seen them". Mawgan replied as he put his arm around Arthur.

"Willy told me my daddy's with the mermaids". Amy said with a glow on her face.

"Tamasine stood up and picked Amy up and cuddled her in. "You little dear". She said.

"Tis funny *tis* always the men that see *em".* Lilly was still laughing.

Tamasine Laughed as she said. "My mum always said it was the rum that saw them not the men".

"If my Father is with them, how can it be the rum? Arthur asked.

Lilly caught hold of Arthur's hand. *"Tis* the angel's your Father is with, that's where all good men go". Lilly leaned forward and kissed him on the check.

After a little more chat about mermaids and rum. Mawgan, Tamasine, and the children, made their way home.

It had been agreed that Tamasine and the children would stay at Mawgan's whilst he was away. The children were quite excited about it as they could go down on the beach and play, and Rajah and Willy were always around they were all very fond of each other.

Winnie hadn't been down to Mawgan's for almost a week she knew that it would only end in an argument about James. But no way could she let Mawgan go on his trip without her wishing him good luck. So on Tuesday morning after James had left for Penzance Winnie made her way down to Mawgan's. "Have you been hiding from us" .Mawgan asked as Winnie entered the cottage.

"O you know what it's like with James and that". Winnie replied with a bit of a sigh.

"No I don't know, anyway how is the smuggler catcher doing". Mawgan asked in a sarcastic tone.

"Please Mawgan don't, he is only doing what he thinks is right. And besides if he didn't do the job someone else would. Who knows what would happen then". Winnie wanted to reassure Mawgan that James was a good man.

"Whatever James does you must never stay away from us I miss you in fact we all do". Mawgan put his arm around her.

"You miss my bed is more like it". Winnie smiled.

"Don't you?" Mawgan replied in a whisper as he pulled her in tight to him.

"God yes no one could ever make love like you do, but sometimes we have to give up a little pleasure for love". Winnie put her arms around Mawgan they both pulled each other in so tight that there whole bodies where touching.

"I don't see why we can't have both". Mawgan whispered as he kissed her neck.

"I think we should stop before we do something we will both regret". Winnie replied but making no effort to break away.

"What would there be to regret". Mawgan broke away and started to undo Winnie's dress from the top and slipping his hand in side.

"Mawgan this is so wrong". Winnie whispered as she started to undo the rest of her buttons. "I don't want you to stop until you have made love to me".

"Mawgan took his hand back, I can't do this, I'm sorry it's not right, God I want you but it's so wrong". Mawgan walked to the other side of the room.

"Why! Is it Tamasine we all know how much you want her but it has never stopped you before". Winnie started to do her buttons up.

"Yes Tamasine part of it, but it's you and James it's just not right, your his now". Mawgan opened the door and stood in the door way.

"I'm nobodies". Winnie said as she came over to the door and put her arm around Mawgan's shoulder. "I just hope Tamasine appreciates what she has". She whispered in Mawgan's ear.

"I think it's more about me appreciating what I could have, and no way am I going to lose it before I have it". Mawgan said as he walked outside.

"That doesn't make sense how can you lose something if you haven't got it". Winnie followed Mawgan outside.

"Trust me you can. Now let's just give Willy a shout to make a pot of tea and we can sit out here and chat about you and James". Mawgan wanted to pretend what had just happened never did.

Winnie smiled, "I'll make the tea". She leaned forwarded and kissed Mawgan on the check "Mawgan you will always be a special man to me she said, as she made her way back inside to make a pot tea.

Chapter 15

On the Wednesday Captain Pendray and his crew set sail from the Quay.

It was now Friday morning everyone was up early for it was the day Mawgan was to set sail. Mawgan would not sail until two in the afternoon due to the tides. So a large breakfast feast was arranged with Tamasine and the children. Winnie came down when James had left for Penzance; even Lilly-Rose had made her way up to Mawgan's cottage. Everyone would miss Mawgan when he was gone and they were certainly making it known. Suddenly there was a knock on the door. Winnie who was closes to the door opened it. "I was looking for Captain Mawgan". A woman's voice said nervously.

"Mrs Penrose". Mawgan exclaimed.

"O Captain I'm sorry to turn up like this, but I don't know where to turn and you did say if ever I needed help to look you up". Mrs Penrose was shaking as she talked.

"Now now just calm down and come in and tell me what troubles you so". Mawgan put his arm around her and led her in to the cottage.

"It's Samuel; my Father caught him in my house he had him beaten up, now my Father says he is a thief and has put a warrant on him with a fifty pound reward. I know if he is caught my father will have him hung". She was sounding so upset.

"Is he a thief?" Tamasine asked.

"He is an honest caring man; all he wants is to spend his life with me, can that be so bad". Mrs Penrose was so upset.

"Where's Samuel now?" Mawgan asked.

"He is outside I just need some where for him to hide until we find away to be together". There was a real plea for help in her voice.

"You better get him to come in". Mawgan replied.

Mrs Penrose went out she was gone for what seemed several minutes as Samuel was hiding as he was afraid to trust anyone, when they did both enter the cottage the scares were still there evident of the ferocious beating he must have taken. So much so that everyone gasped when they saw him.

"Gosh your face it needs treatment". Winnie exclaimed.

"He should come down to my house". Lilly-Rose said as she ran her hand over his face.

"Were can we hide him". Tamasine asked she knew they had to do something and with Mawgan going away it would be difficult.

"I think he should join me on our trip". Mawgan said as he looked at Mrs Penrose. "We will be away for several months mind". He continued.

"Can he I don't no ware you are going but if it keeps Samuel safe then please, yes take him with you". Mrs Penrose was full of anxiety.

Suddenly little Arthur came forward. "Excuse Me". He said politely "If you are Mrs Penrose, did you know my Father". Tamasine had told him he was a gallant man he was Admiral Penrose. Arthur caught hold of Amy's hand and went over beside her.

"Yes dear I knew him and he was a truly gallant man, and I know he was very proud of you two, and you must call me Aunty Damaris" .Mrs Penrose bent down and picked Amy up.

"Does that go for all of us". Winnie asked.

"What call me Aunty"? Mrs Penrose smiled there was a sense of relief on her face she knew she was amongst friends.

"If we just called you Damaris". Winnie smiled back.

Tamasine put her arm around Damaris, "What about you what will you do".

"I'm not sure I will have to go back to my house tonight" .Damaris paused then continued. "I want to sort Henry's affairs out before I leave; my Father is making it very difficult. I so much want these two to have what is rightfully theirs". She had now knelt down beside Arthur still with Amy in her arms; they could all see she was a caring woman.

"Do you think it safe for you to go back?" Samuel said as he knelt down beside Damaris and the children.

"Mawgan went over to Winnie, "I don't think you should mention any of this to James". He said quietly.

Damaris heard what he had said. "Who is James"? She asked.

"James Wilmot Brown he is my lodger he is a revenue man". Winnie said quite causally.

"I have heard my Father speak of him, he mentions him he says he is a true servant to the King, I believe my Father pays him through some associates in Plymouth". She was now worried again.

"Don't worry about James he says his job is to catch smugglers not fugitives, besides I won't mention any of this to him". Winnie was quite reassuring.

"I'm afraid we have to get down to the ship now". Mawgan said he turned to Samuel. "And you my friend should spend an hour with Lilly-Rose before we sail so that you can get those wounds sorted". Mawgan taped Samuel on the shoulder as he said it.

They all got up and made their way down to the quay Samuel went in to Lilly-Rose's cottage. Willy had told Mawgan that he would ride to Bodmin with Damaris. As they all stood on the quay watching Mawgan and the crew get the ship ready, Winnie stood beside Tamasine "I hope you showed Mawgan how much love you have for him before he left". She whispered.

"Mawgan knows how I feel". She replied with a note of mind your own business in her voice.

"He might know how you feel, but my question was have you shown him". Winnie would not let the matter drop.

"I will show him when the time is right". Tamasine replied angrily.

"I hope for your sake it won't be too late". Winnie said as she turned and walked away.

It did not seem long before Samuel came down with Lilly-Rose, it looked as if a miracle had been preformed you could hardly see a mark on his face. He Kissed Damaris good bye and climbed aboard the ship. Willy then left with Damaris as she had to get back to Bodmin hopefully before dark. There was just Lilly-Rose, Tamasine and the children left on the quay when they casted off.

"You seem troubled my child". Lilly-Rose said to Tamasine as the ship sailed out of sight.

"O it's just what Winnie said". Tamasine shrugged he shoulders.

"Winnie hey, and what did she say".

"She asked if I showed Mawgan how much I loved him before he left". Tamasine replied with a bit of a sulk.

"Did you get in is bed she meant". Lilly-Rose laughed, "Well did you".

Tamasine blushed, "No". She said softly.

"Good he has something to look forward to when he gets back". Lilly replied with a smile.

"O Lilly I do love you". Tamasine put her arm around her and kissed her on the check.

They both laughed as they walked up to Lilly's cottage, where they parted company and Tamasine and the children made their way back to Mawgan's cottage where they would be staying until his return.

Mawgan and his crew had only just got out of Mounts bay when they were surrounded by five naval ships, a voice from the bridge of one of the ships shouted. "Captain Mawgan lower your main sail we are going to board you".

One of the crew members came up to Mawgan. "What do we do captain?" He asked.

"We let them board we have no choice". Mawgan replied showing little fear this is no more than he expected.

Samuel came up to Mawgan. "It's me they want I can't put you and your crew in jeopardy, I will jump ship". Samuel climbed on to the side.

"You will do no such thing, go down and look like you are working in the galley". Mawgan said as he pulled Samuel back by the shoulder. "It's not you they want". He whispered.

A rowing boat approached with about ten men in, all but one had riffles pointing upwards. As they got close Mawgan threw a rope ladder over the side. "How can I help you?" He asked the man without a riffle.

"We have reason to believe you are smuggling ore to one of our country's enemy's". The man replied quite sternly.

Mawgan laughed out load. "My dear man my ship is unlaiden I have to go abroad to seek work for her".

"Then you will have no problem with me searching her hold". The man replied.

"Help yourself". Mawgan had a smile of contentment on his face.

It wasn't long before the man stormed back on deck. "My apologizes captain". He said. "I think we have been taken for fools". The man left the ship in somewhat of a rage.

"Come on hoist that main sail; let's get under way Mawgan shouted after the men had left.

Chapter 16

Several days passed and then Mawgan meet up with his other ship off Spain, they sailed in to harbour together. Just as they where tying up not really knowing if they would be welcome or not a man approached Mawgan instantly recognised him as his father's old friend.

"Thank god a friendly face". Mawgan chuckled as he held his hand out for the man to shake.

"What brings you to these parts; you have never sailed all this way to see me". The man replied.

"O I have". Mawgan continued to tell the man all about Lord Tremeldon how he had stopped his ships working, and how he had sailed with ship and ore to sale.

"You English and you're Lords". The man replied with a laugh he put his hand on Mawgan's shoulder. "You remind me so much of your Father. "This is something he would have done".

"Well can you help me?" Mawgan asked.

"Of course my friend, come we will go to my bank, I assume you want gold". The man had suggested no price.

"How much is it all worth". Mawgan concerned no price had been mentioned.

"I dealt with your father for many years, every time I came to England he bought many of things from me, and at no time did we discuss money. I always took what he gave me and found him to be fair. I hope you will trust me to do the same, good friends never discuss money". He held his hand out for Mawgan to shake.

Mawgan took his hand and gave a firm hand shake. "I trust any friend of father's".

They walked through the streets which had a strong smell of fish men sat in groups drinking small vessels of coffee, there were women mending nets mixed in with women of ill repute. The whole place had a buzz about it, yet calm. They got to the bank Mawgan waited outside for the man who soon returned with a small bag of gold, and tossed it to Mawgan who never even tried to guess the weight he just put it inside his shirt.

They walked back to the ships; the two crews had now united on Mawgan's ship and ready to sail. The two men said there good bye's and Mawgan climbed on board and they set sail next stop India.

Chapter 17

It had been two weeks since Mawgan had left Cornwall. It was a bright autumn day Tamasine had just finished giving the children there breakfast.

Willy came in to the cottage from the stable at the back he had been getting a horse and cart ready to go to Combe farm and get some hay.

"I thought young Arthur would like to come with me". He said as he picked up a piece of bread from the table.

"Can I"? Arthur shouted excitedly.

Amy got down from the table and ran over to Willy and caught hold his hand.

"O you want to come to do you?" Willy bent down and picked her up.

Amy just nodded.

"Are you sure" Tamasine said with a note of concern.

"They'll be all right, don't *E* worry I'll keep *um* safe". Willy took another piece of bread from the table.

"Well if your sure I can do a bit of washing, where's Rajah, I bet he has a stack of washing to be done". Tamasine took two coats of a peg behind the door and put them on the children.

"Rajah's out back cleaning out the stables, *ell be* stinking. I tell *en* he should go down Lowenna's, but *e* sooner go in the sea, maze I call *en*". Willy laughed and picked Amy up and carried her out and put her on the cart. Arthur followed and climbed up his self.

Tamasine came out and waved good bye, she had no concerns that Arthur would be all right as he often went with Willy, but Amy very rarely left her side.

"See *E drekly"*. Willy shouted as they trotted up the lane.

Tamasine had not long returned inside and was about to shout to Rajah when a knock came one the door. Tamasine opened it an there dressed in white trousers frilly shirt riding jacket boots up to just below the knees, and carrying a riding whip in his hand with it placed across one shoulder was Albert Stoneham.

"Mawgan is away". Tamasine said somewhat surprised to see him.

"I know!! He made me look a fool". Came the reply as Albert pushed his way in to the cottage.

"If you know then what business do you have here?"

"I think I need to be repaid for my losses". Albert was now in the cottage looking at the painting of Tamasine as a Mermaid. "Tell me when you posed for this". Albert asked pointing to the painting with his whip.

"I didn't pose for it".

"O really perhaps I should see if the painting is true to life". Albert had now turned towards Tamasine and rested the end of his whip in her cleavage.

"I would like you to leave now Sir". Tamasine had a nervous quiver in her voice.

"O my dear I am not going any ware, not until I have been repaid in one way or another".

"I have no money". Tamasine stuttered.

"Then we will have to think of another way wont we!!" Albert smirked.

"You're making me feel uncomfortable, would you please leave". Tamasine tried to say it firmly.

"You should just relax my dear". Albert put his whip in between two buttons on the top of Tamasine's dress and pulled hard two buttons came flying out exposing more of her breasts.

"Get out". Tamasine shouted as she leaned forward and slapped him hard across the face.

"You shouldn't have done that". Albert wiped the side of his face; he caught hold of Tamasine's arms and pushed her back against the table. He leaned forwarded and kissed what breasts were exposed Tamasine was wriggling trying to get away. He brought his head up to try and kiss her, Tamasine spat in his face.

"You bitch". Albert shouted as he left her arms go and hit her hard on the face first one side then the other. He then caught hold of each side of her dress and pulled hard all the buttons came flying out exposing all the front of her body. Albert then grabbed her by the throat with one hand and pushed her hard turning her by the throat until she fell to the floor.

As she fell to the floor she pulled her dress back over her. "Please go please go she whimpered". As she started to crawl across the floor.

"I'm going no ware". Albert bent down and pulled Tamasine back to the middle of the room. He put a leg each side of her and started to undo his trousers, Tamasine pulled her leg back and mustered as much strength as she could and brought her foot up as hard as she could kicking Albert between his legs he doubled over with pain. She managed to get up and staggered to the door at the back of the cottage and shouted to Rajah, who soon came running.

As Rajah entered the cottage he could see what was happening and he stood in front of Tamasine as Albert approached her.

"Out of my way". Albert shouted as he went to pull Rajah away.

Rajah clinched his fist and punched Albert hard, then another and another, until he was begging him to stop.

Rajah dragged Albert out who had blood spouting from his nose and mouth; he got him to his horse. "Don't you ever go near her again". Rajah said quite calmly as Albert struggled on to his horse rather dazed.

"You will regret this". Albert shouted as his horse bolted up the road after Rajah had slapped its back.

Tamasine had made herself quite descent when Rajah came back in to the cottage, "did he". Rajah paused then "you know!!"

"No but he would have if you hadn't come in when you did". Tamasine was sobbing.

"I don't think he will be back again". Rajah was trying to reassure her.

Tamasine went over to a cupboard and took out a long case; she opened it and took out two pistols. "I hope he comes back". She held one pistol in each hand and Rajah knew what she was thinking.

"That would get you hung". He said as he took the pistols out of her hand.

"I would sooner be hung then let that bastard have his way with me".

"Why don't you go up and see Winnie for a while until the children come back". Rajah didn't really know what to say.

With that the door started to open Tamasine picked one of the pistols up and pointed it to the door, suddenly Winnie appeared she jumped feet to see a pistol pointed at her. "I only came down to ask who the handsome man was that galloped up the road, he seemed to be in a rather hurry".

"Don't let looks fool you; the man is no better than on of Willy's pigs". Tamasine said as she put the pistol down and started to tell Winnie what had happened.

"God you shouldn't have fought him he might have killed you". Winnie said in a concerning way.

"I would have rather have died than give in to that big oaf". Tamasine replied.

"That's where we differ". Winnie smiled. "I don't like pain, I would sooner someone put something in a place it was meant to go in than I would die".

"Winnie Trewin you got no morals. That's all us women have that we can call our own, and it should not be given up lightly". Tamasine flopped down in a chair.

"I don't think we should just let anyone, but preacher Jack always say's we should share our possession". Winnie laughed.

"You can make a joke of it, but I will always be a one man's women". Tamasine insisted.

"I have to go now". Winnie said. "But just let me give you a bit of advice, don't let yourself get old and wrinkly before you give it, if you're waiting for love it might never come".

"O it will!! That's one thing I'm sure of". Tamasine's face had now lit up.

Just as Winnie was leaving, Willy returned with the children who were quite excited about their trip. Tamasine told Willy all about Albert Stoneham.

"I should go and teach him a lesson". Willy replied.

"I think Rajah done that all right; I don't think he'll bother me again".

Tamasine chuckled.

Chapter 18

A couple of days had passed, James returned to Winnie, and was quite all evening. Winnie knew something was wrong but James would say nothing. Winnie thought she would not press him until they were in bed.

Later that night in her bed, Winnie gently ran her fingers through James's hair, she then kissed him passionately. "Tell me darling what is troubling you." She whispered as her hand wonder down across his body to parts that might make any a man talk.

"I can't tell you, you won't want me here anymore if I did" .James was sounding quite sad.

"I can't just turn my love of because you tell me something I don't like; you should tell me it might make things easier for you". Winnie kissed his chest between every word she said.

James pushed her up and sat up. "I have to apprehend Rajah tomorrow". He blurted out.

"Why you know he's no smuggler". Winnie looked surprised.

"I know but I have instructions, there are three men coming from Truro who will later take him on to Bristol, and then on to London he is to be treated as an enemy of the crown". James was talking quite serious.

"You said you had no interest in Rajah when you came here you said you where just interested in people that evaded duty". Winnie got out of bed and picked up a robe and put on.

"That was true but if the people that pay me give me other tasks then I have to do them, the law has to be kept". James got out of bed and pulled his trousers on.

"I just don't understand this law of yours who makes them; Rajah has broken no law here". Winnie sat down in a chair and put her head in her hands.

"I know it's difficult for you to understand but if we didn't have laws it would be like anakey people doing what they like; the country would be run by gangs". James sat down beside her and caught hold her hand.

"Isn't that what's happening now? The country run by rich gangs, if you got money then you got power over people". Winnie pulled her hand away from James's.

"What do you want me to do; I have to do my job, do you want me to go". James again caught hold of her hand.

"I don't want you to go, but I just wish I could understand you, why can't you just say no to capturing Rajah". Winnie stood up and looked at James and said. "I just want you to be one of us".

"One of you". James smiled. "And what does that entail".

Winnie thought for a moment, then sighed and said, "I suppose the easy way to describe us is people that look out for one another". She then paused and continued. "O we also live and let live".

"It sound's idyllic but it won't survive without laws". James went back to the bed.

"Well let me tell you James Wilmot Sparrow we have managed all right up to now". Winnie smiled as she removed her robe and climbed in to the bed beside him.

It was five thirty the next morning, Winnie gently got out of bed not disturbing James she slipped on her robe and gently opened the door. She ran down the lane as fast as she could to Mawgan's cottage where Tamasine was staying. She banged loud on the door until Tamasine appeared.

"What is it, do you know what time it is". Tamasine said as she whipped her eyes. Winnie explained that she had to be quick as she had sneaked out. She told her how James was going to take Rajah in to custody in the morning.

Winnie left Tamasine and ran up the road to her cottage gently opened the door and sneaked in dropped her robe to the floor and climbed in to bed. James eyes were still shut but it looked like he had a smile on his face, he knew were Winnie had been. He hoped deep down Rajah would be gone.

104

When Winnie had gone Tamasine went and woke Rajah and Willy up. "I should leave immediately". Rajah. said.

"You won't get anywhere out there on your own trying to hide, we can hide you here with the imports". Tamasine looked at Willy for agreement.

"That's right you will be safer here". Willy said.

"I cannot put you and the children in danger; I must leave and take my chances". Rajah got out of his bed and reached for his trousers.

"Come on Willy you must get out". Tamasine said as she went over and started to pull the bed cloths of him.

"But Miss Tamasine". Willy started to say but to late Tamasine soon learned why he didn't get right out as his hands went down to cover his modesty.

"O I'm sorry I never thought". Tamasine said with a laugh, "Now come on we must get on.

Tamasine went back down in to the main room in the cottage she took the pistols out of there box again as she waited for Willy and Rajah to join her. "How do these things work?" She asked Willy as he entered the room.

"Miss Tamasine put *um* down you should' *en* play with *um*". Willy said as he took the pistols out of her hand.

"Willy!" I'm not playing now show me, are they loaded". Tamasine was quite forceful.

Willy took one of the pistols from Tamasine; he took a small horn of powder out of the case and tipped some down the barrel, and rammed it down with a small rod from the case. He then took a small lead shot out of a small cloth bag and put it down the barrel which he then rammed down.

"Now this one". Tamasine said as she handed Willy the other pistol.

Willy reluctantly took it and loaded it. "Just don't *E* do anything silly with *um*, they can kill". He said as he handed Tamasine the second one.

Tamasine turned to Rajah. "You must hide now before the children wake we will have to tell them that you have gone". Tamasine was thinking of every possibility that could go wrong.

Seven, eight, nine, ten o clock came around and no sign of James and his men.

Willy started to get a bit concerned as he was supposed to take a ham and some tea over to preacher jack's, as he was holding a service followed by lunch for the women whose men were at sea.

"You go I will be all right". Tamasine insisted.

Willy had only been gone around ten minutes when there was a knock on the door. Tamasine could see out the small side window that Albert Stoneham was outside sat on his horse. She picked up one of the pistols and held it behind her back, she slowly opened the door. Standing in the doorway was James.

"Good morning Miss Tamasine, we have come to arrest Rajah". James said politely.

"I'm afraid he's not here he left a few days ago, in fact the day that bastard on the horse came around". She replied loudly so that Albert would here.

"Sorry to have troubled you". James replied turning to walk away.

Another man pushed James to one side. "That's not good enough let's ask the kid there if he knows where he is". He said as he stood in the door way.

Tamasine took a few steps backwards until she was in front of Arthur and Amy; she brought the pistol around from behind her back. She held it straight out in front of her, her hand shook as she pulled the hammer back, just like Willy had shown her. "Take one step near the children and I will pull the trigger". She said nervously her whole body trembling.

The man just laughed and made a steep towards her. Tamasine's hand trembled that much that she unwittingly pulled the trigger, the led shot wised by his head taking a piece of his ear with it.

The man's hand immediately went to his ear that was bleeding; Tamasine dropped the pistol on the table and picked up the other one. She held it out straight this time there was no shaking in her hand. "This time my aim is two inches to the right". She said quite calmly.

The man immediately turned and went out the door closing it behind him in a terrified way.

106

Albert Stoneham called James over to him. "Tell me don't you think we should search the place". He said as he dismounted from his horse.

"I see no reason, if Miss Tamasine say's Rajah's not there then I'm sure that to be true". James in no way wanted any of them to enter the cottage.

"You sure you haven't told that wench of yours to warn them?"Albert rested his whip on James's shoulder as he asked the question.

"Sir I hope you are not questioning my loyalty to your Father and are King". James said it a way that no one would doubt.

"I would never question your loyalty to my Father and the King, but I have to ask if you are loyal to me". Albert removed his whip from James's shoulder.

"Sir if you're aim is to uphold the law then I am loyal to you". James stepped back from Albert.

"Good man now why don't you take a couple of men with you and go on the beach and search the caves. I'll take the others with me and we will take the lane". Albert made a gesture to two of the men to go with James.

Albert and the others made their way along the lane, the where about half way between the last cottage and the chapel when they met Willy coming the other way. "Good morning". Albert said. "We are looking for an Indian chap, do you know of his whereabouts'".

"Afraid I can't *elp E*". Willy said nervously.

"Tell me where do you live, would you be Mawgan's peasant?"Albert asked.

"I sir". Willy again replied nervously.

"Then you must know the Indian". Albert brought his horse whip down hard on the side of Willy's face then calmly said. "Perhaps we should start again, now do you know the Indian".

Willy put his hand up to his face blood was running down his check. "I did know *im* but *E* left some days ago". He replied.

Again Albert dismounted from his horse, brought his whip down across Willy's face in a real fit of temper, he then put his face so close to Willy's it was almost touching. "Why don't I believe you?"He said.

"*Tis* true I can tell *E* no more". Willy replied his face num with pain.

Albert turned to the men that were with him. "Perhaps you would like to explain to our friend here that we like to be told the truth". One man came forwarded and caught Willy hold by the arms, another stepped forward and punched him hard in the stomach once then again and again Willy was doubled over in pain. Albert came over and lifted Willy's head by the hair and calmly asked. "Where's the Indian?"

"I don't know sir". Willy just managed say.

"O I think you do". Albert beckoned to the men to hit him some more.

One of the men again punched and punched Willy, the man that was holding Willy let his arms go and he dropped to the ground. The man then knelt down beside Willy. "I think he's dead". He said.

Albert came over and looked down at Willy. "Kick him in the ditch". He calmly said.

Albert and the men then went on to the chapel; he calmly opened the door which creaked loudly as he did so. The chapel had about a dozen women and a preacher in side. "Good morning ladies". Albert said as he turned and acknowledged the preacher.

"Good morning". Came a sort of muffled reply.

"We are looking for an Indian chap has any of you seen him". Albert asked.

"Would that be Rajah?" The preacher asked.

"You know the man do you". Albert made his way over to the preacher.

"Yes but he hasn't been around for a day or two". The preacher replied.

Willy had told the preacher and the woman that people were coming to capture Rajah.

One of the women suddenly shouted. "I've seen him".

Albert went over beside her. "And were might that be my dear?" He asked.

"Let me see was it yesterday or the day before, I was on the quay in Penzance when I saw him getting on a ship". The women said.

"What where you doing in Penzance? Surely you must know what day it was". Albert was trying to keep calm.

"I go there every day Sir my man's ship should be home any day I go every day to see if it's in". The women sounded so convincing.

"Thank you ladies". Albert said as he beckoned to his men and the left the chapel.

As they left one of the men said. "It appears we have missed him".

"I think you are right, I suggest you find James and call the search off". Albert mounted his horse and galloped off.

Chapter 19

Almost three hours had passed since Albert and his men had visited Mawgan's cottage, and Tamasine started to get concerned about Willy's whereabouts. She got the children, and made her way towards the chapel. It was young Arthur that stumbled across Willy as he was running in the gutters. He quickly shouted to Tamasine who ran over and pulled him out on to the lane, he was covered in blood and not moving.

"Is he dead?" Arthur asked.

Tamasine put her head down to Willy's. "No he is breathing but only just". She turned to Arthur, "I want you to be a big boy run down to Winnie's and tell her to come quickly".

Arthur ran down the road as fast as he could, he had only been gone a few seconds when Tamasine could hear someone coming towards her singing. She shouted for help and Lowenna and two of her girls appeared.

"Whatever is it?" Lowenna shouted back still too far away to see Willy on the floor.

"It's Willy he's been hurt".

Lowenna came running over. "God who done this". She asked.

Winnie had now come on the scene. "Your bloody James is responsible for this". Tamasine shouted.

"I don't believe James had anything to do with it". Winnie replied angrily.

"Nothing like this ever happened until James came here, now people are afraid to do anything". Tamasine was still shouting.

"What about you if you weren't so high and mighty about your bloody body, Albert Stoneham would never have come looking for Rajah. This is all about you, its called revenge". Winnie was sounding as angry as Tamasine to think she could blame James.

"Stop it both of you. You aren't doing Willy any favours, the only people to blame are the people that have done this". Lowenna said as she had her arm around Willy's head.

"Your right". Winnie replied. "Now we have to get him back to the cottage".

"No" Lowenna said. "We will take him to my place; me and my girls will nurse him. If he is going to die I know where he would want to die".

"I think you are probably right". Tamasine raised a little smile as she was sure she could see a smile on Willy's face.

One of Lowenna's girls was wearing a long heavy coat. Lowenna told her to take it off she then laid it on the road and they manage to get Willy on to it. Four of them caught hold of a corner each and carried Willy down to Lowenna's. Tamasine and the children went with them. "Are you coming?" Lowenna asked Winnie.

"No I'm going to look for James; I don't believe he had anything to do with it. But if he did he won't be coming home to my place". Winnie was determined to get to the bottom of what happened.

Winnie decided to walk towards Penzance as she knew that's were James would have gone. She had only gone a couple of miles when she could see James and the rest of the men involved in the search coming up from the beach, she ran over to them, "Tell me". She shouted "You had nothing to do with it".

"Do with what". James asked with a look of surprise.

"It's Willy he has been beaten up, he is close to death". Winnie could see that James had no idea of what she was talking about.

Three of the men just smirked James approached one. "What do you know of this?" He asked quite forcefully.

The man just laughed and turned away. James pulled him around towards him by the shoulder. "Tell me". He shouted.

"He should have told us what we wanted". The man replied as he surged his shoulders.

James turned to Winnie. "Where is he?" He asked. "Take me to him".

Winnie took James down to Lowenna's. Willy had still not come around. "Does this make you happy?" Lowenna asked as James looked down at Willy.

"Of course not". James replied as he put his hand down in front of Willy's nose. "Thank god he's breathing".

"Tell me why would someone do this, everyone knows he wouldn't harm anyone". Lowenna sat down on the bed beside Willy and stroked his head.

"I must go and see Tamasine; she has to know that I had nothing to do with this". James caught hold of Winnie's hand. "Will you come with me"? He asked

The pair of them left and made their way to Mawgan's cottage, when they got there Tamasine was sat at the table ramming powder down the barrels of the pistols.

"What are you doing?" Winnie asked.

"I need you to look after the children for me". Tamasine replied calmly.

"Why where are you going". Winnie asked.

"I am going to kill the bastard, that done that to Willy". Tamasine picked up the led shot and rammed it down the barrel with such force; She then dropped the pistols on the table, dropped her head in her hands and burst in to tears.

Winnie sat down beside her and put her arm around her; James came over and picked up the pistols. "This isn't the way". He said.

Winnie looked up. "Then you tell me James bloody Wilmot Sparrow what is the way, to deal with bastards like that".

"I'm not sure, I know you're angry as we all are, but I know this is not the way". James put the pistols back in there case.

"Do you see know how we all think your idea of law is wrong". Tamasine sad to James as she wiped a tear from her cheek.

"You can't think this is my Idea of law". James replied.

"I know you had nothing to do with it. But the people that pay you did". Tamasine replied quite angrily.

"You said you wanted to get revenue for the government, well tell me how much have you collected?" Tamasine asked as she completely dried her eyes.

"I don't see how that is relevant to the situation". James replied.

"I'll tell you how it's relevant. Every shilling you collect means someone starves. People say that since you have been in Penzance, more people are starving because they are afraid to do anything so you aren't collecting any revenue from them or anyone else, so what's it all for, absolutely nothing that's what". Tamasine had tears starting to run down her cheek again.

"They are robbing our country of its revenue and whatever happens, that cannot be right, and that has nothing to do with what has happened here today". James wanted to distinguish one from the other.

"Nonsense who done this, the son of one of the people that pay you, that's who. Just answer me two questions, is Samuel Hocking one of the men that pay's you". Tamasine paused.

James answered. "Yes if you mean the merchant".

"O I mean the merchant, now tell me have you raided the Carters place". Mawgan had always talked about the Carters and how they sold a lot of contraband to Samuel Hocking.

"No I have no evidence to look in to their business I have it from good authority that they run a legitimate business". James replied.

"By who? I bet you have had orders not to go near them."Tamasine stood up and put her face close to James's.

"Its really no concern of yours but it was Samuel Hocking, that told me he knows the family".

"I bet he did. Let me tell you. You would get more revenue in one raid then you have in every one you have ever done in Penzance". Tamasine's face was still close to James.

"I can't do that without permission as I have been told I must not operate outside Penzance". James replied.

"Exactly, you won't get permission because your so called law men benefit from them, now let's just leave it at that. I have to tend to the children then go down and see Willy". Tamasine picked Amy up who had been playing on the floor.

James and Winnie left, James knew what he was doing everyone didn't agree with but he believed that what he was doing was right. Not for the people that where paying him as he was learning what rogues they were, but he believed it right for the country.

The Idea of going to Falmouth with her pistols had deserted Tamasine for the moment, as she and the children were going down to Lowenna's. On the way they meet Lilly-Rose who had heard about Willy and his injury. "I will walk down to Lowenna's with you". She said as she got up from her seat outside her cottage.

"Why can't James see what he is doing is so wrong". Tamasine asked the wise old lady.

"Is he so wrong my dear? After all he is only doing what he believes is to be right". Lilly said as they made their way down the road.

"How can it be right to penalise the poor while the rich get away with murder". Tamasine would never understand.

"My dear life has always been like that. We all know how horrible some of these so called wealthy people can be, we also know how a lot of them got their wealth. I know what a lot of ordinary people have to do to feed their children. I also know that there has to be laws and some we will never like". Lilly was trying to get Tamasine to see things different.

"I know your right. It's just that James is such a nice bloke I feel he shouldn't be doing what he's doing". Tamasine was so serious.

"Well I would sooner he was the one doing the job rather than some bloody lout like the ones that Willy came across". Lilly said as they reached Lowenna's.

"I do agree with you there, I just don't know what to think any more, I sometimes think I am blaming others when I should be blaming myself. If I had let that bastard have his way with me then none of this would have happened and Willy wouldn't have been hurt". Tamasine opened Lowenna's door.

Lilly put her hand on her shoulder just stopping her from going in. "You must not think like that, no man has a right to any women keeping your dignity is something you should be proud of whatever the outcome. You know what's wrong with you, you are missing Mawgan". Lilly took her hand of her shoulder to let her go on in.

Tamasine whispered. "I do miss him I wonder where he is now".

Chapter 20

Mawgan had sailed from Spain and was at his first port of call in India. The idea is for Mawgan not to go ashore here but to send Captain Pendray and the rest of the crew. Mawgan gave Captain Pendray some gold to buy cargo to take back to Cornwall.

Mawgan hadn't shaved since he left Cornwall because at their next port of call he would change in to Captain Walter Dark.

They were in port for two days, and when they left their ship the Kernow Mist was laden with goods of all description, they ranged from carpets and fabrics to tea and herbs just to name a few.

The ship sailed on up the coast to Delia whilst sailing they removed the ships name Kernow Mist and replaced it with HMS Action. Mawgan had a bottle of red dye that Lilly- Rose had given him which he put on his hair and beard.

They sailed in to port and after tying up alongside, Mawgan went ashore armed with the letter that he got Henri to forge and using the name Captain Walter Dark.

He walked through the dock until he could find someone he thought looked a little important. "Could you tell me where I could find the Governor General"? He asked.

"Is he expecting you?" The man replied in an Indian accent.

"Yes I think so". Mawgan knew he wasn't.

"You say you think so, is he or isn't he. I don't think it a difficult question?" The man was obvesley someone of authority.

"I would need to know who I'm speaking to before I disclose delicate information". Mawgan was sounding as important as the man.

"I am Mr. Sherriff I am the secretary to the Governor General and I serve King Georg of the world". The man replied in an excited Indian voice.

"Well Mr Sherriff I don't think the empire quite stretches the whole world, but like you I serve the king, and I take my orders directly from him". Mawgan took the letter out of his pocket and showed the man the royal seal.

"Then I will take you to the Governor Sir. The man held his hand out for Mawgan to lead on.

They walked for about ten minutes until they came to a large house with a large veranda. There were a number of people sitting on it, there was also half a dozen young women dressed in silk trousers and tops with their midriff exposed they were waving large fans over what looked like very well to do people. The men were dressed in expensive suites, and the women in dresses that Mawgan had never seen the like before.

Mr Sherriff walked up the steps of the veranda where an elderly Gentlemen sat. "This man has a letter from the king Governor". He said excitedly.

"And you are". The elderly man asked.

"Captain Walter Dark of his majesty's service". Mawgan did a little bow.

"So you are the notorious captain a lot of merchant men have been talking about. They say you and your men are worth more than ten army's". The governor lit a large cigar.

"I do have a proud fighting force, but ten army's, that could be a bit of exaggeration". Mawgan smiled.

"And why do we have your pleasure? The Governor asked.

"I am looking for a girl". Mawgan calmly replied.

"Well we can help you there you can take your pick of any one of these". The governor held his arm out and moved it around in the circle pointing out the women with the fans.

"No it is a particular girl I want". Mawgan nervously handed the Governor the letter that Henri had produced.

The Governor read it. "Annabel you have come all this way for Annabel". The governor was sounding surprised.

"No Sir we had a disturbance to put down not a million miles away". Mawgan had rehearsed answers to the questions he might be asked.

"And where might that have been". The governor had heard of no trouble.

"I'm afraid one of the orders I received, was to tell no one of our mission, and I'm afraid that does include you Sir. So I hope you will forgive me if I say no more on this matter". Mawgan hoped that would be an end to the questions.

"I do not doubt the authority you have in your possession, but what I don't understand two days ago I received notice that the Earl of Westmoorland is on his way out here. Louie the French man is bringing him he is to make arrangements with his daughter. You see she is to marry my son on his return from America which won't be long now the rebellion has been quashed". The Governor looked quite pleased.

"I'm afraid you have false information Sir America is all but lost Spain has signed a pack with the rebels and are firing on our troops. The earl of Westmoorland was on his way here but after discussion with the King, he has asked to see Annabel before her marriage. So that's why I'm here". Mawgan was getting nervous, the simple sail in pick her up and go, was now not looking quite so easy.

"Well I'm afraid Annabel is away at the moment I'm not sure if she will be back tomorrow, so why don't you let your men come ashore. I'm sure a drink or two would be appreciated, and we could even supply a woman or two, I'm sure there are a few of your crew that are missing home comforts". The Governor chuckled.

"My men are a fighting force they nether drink nor undertake foliations with a woman that might leave them week for days. So they will stay on board and I will stay with them". Mawgan didn't know what to do now.

"They said you are a hard man, and you treat your men in that way so I will wish you good day and we will speak tomorrow". The Governor stood up and held his hand out for Mawgan to shake.

Mawgan returned to his ship and explained to the crew what had happened. "What are we going to do now sail without her"? One of the crew asked.

"We haven't come all this way to return without her". Mawgan replied.

"How, what if the Earl turns up here tomorrow". The crew man asked with a tone of let's get out of here quick.

"I'm not sure how, and we will just have to hope the Earl is far out to sea". Mawgan replied just as a woman's voice shouted up to the ship.

"Good time Mr, Good time". Came a voice over and over again, so much so that in the end Mawgan went up to see her.

"No good time go away". Mawgan said angrily.

"Mr!" The women whispered. "You are looking for Annabel". The women stopped as an official looking man came by. "I want two rubies for good time" .It was obvious the woman was nervous because the man was near.

"Perhaps you should come on board and we can discuss the price for a good time". Mawgan's smile reassured her.

She climbed aboard and went down below Mawgan asked Samuel if he would go up on deck just to keep an eye on the man on the Quay. "Now tell me what you know about Annabel". Mawgan pointed to a chair for her to sit on.

The woman sat down and took a deep breath, she really was quite nervous. She then said. "Annabel is a prisoner she cannot leave her house".

"How do you mean". Mawgan asked.

"She does not want to marry the governor's son she is in love with Rajah who has vanished. Now the Governor has her locked up all the time". The women started to cry.

"Would you be able to take me too her". Mawgan asked.

"Not now Sir it would be too dangerous". It was quite clear that the woman was very frightened.

"Later to night then".

"Meet me midnight in the market. Make sure you are not seen. When I leave you must come up on deck and pay me some money". The women stood up and made her way on to the deck Mawgan followed her, when up on deck the women turned and kissed Mawgan in a long kiss, she then broke away and held her hand out. Mawgan took some coins out of his pocket and dropped them down her cleavage.

Mawgan went down below after he watched her leave.

"I'll come with you tonight Captain". Sam said as Mawgan reached the lower deck.

"I have a bit of a plan, I think we should leave port and anchor out in the bay then row in latter, this would make us less suspicious. First I will go and tell the governor that we will be at anchor in the bay". Mawgan made his way off the ship and up to the Governor's residence.

"You are back so soon Captain". The governor had a look of surprise.

"I just thought I would let you know we are going to anchor out in the bay, I find the temptations here too much for my men. Mawgan said.

"The temptation was already too much for you". The governor chuckled.

"How do you mean". Mawgan frowned.

"Mala is one of my girls, I offered her to you when you were here, but you declined". He took the coins that Mawgan had given the women out of a tin and handed it back to Mawgan. "I will not charge such a man as yourself if you prefer someone a little different then you know where I am. The governor just laughed as Mawgan got up and left.

Mawgan then went back to his ship and they sailed out to the bay. At around ten thirty, four of them got in to a rowing boat and rowed to some rocks. There was a lot of wood floating around. Mawgan and Sam left the boat and clambered ashore Mawgan told the men left behind to collect as much of the wood as possible that was floating close to the shore then take it back to the ship, then bring another boat over to pick them up and get as much wood as possible on that one.

"Do you know where the market is?" Sam whispered.

"No idea". Mawgan replied.

The moon was full as it lit their way up across the rocks and down through the narrow streets a rat or two ran across their path as they approached what looked like rows of stalls all empty. There was the old man sleeping on the floor under a table.

As they walked down through the tables, "Over here". Came a muffled voice.

Standing by a large post in the shadow of the moon was the figure of two women one Mawgan recognised as Mala. They approached the two women who dragged them behind a large canvas that was draped down over one of the stalls.

"This is Annabel". Mala said as she ushered both men in close so they could whisper.

"I thought you were a prisoner". Mawgan was surprised to see her.

"There is only one guard at night and Mala has a way of making him let me out". Annabel looked at Mala and smiled.

"We have come to take you to England and Rajah". Mawgan whispered.

"Is this some sort of trick Rajah is dead, the French man took him, and I was told he was hung". Annabel started to cry.

"Rajah is not dead he is at my place, we rescued him from the French man". Mawgan replied as he put his arm around her.

"Why would you do that?" Annabel was not convinced.

"Why, let's just say he wasn't being treated like a human being". Mawgan smiled at her in a way that would reassure any women. "Now we have to get back to the ship and I hope you will come with us".

"I want Mala to come with us". Annabel replied.

"I'm not sure". Mawgan frowned.

"Please sir I will please you, if I stay they will know I helped Annabel". Mala looked up at Mawgan in a pleading way. "I do very good jig a jig". She whispered.

"That's the last thing I need, jig a jig always gets me in trouble". Mawgan laughed.

"If she can't come then I stay". Annabel said firmly.

"Ok" Mawgan reluctantly replied, as he knew the longer they where there the more danger they were in.

They all made their way back to the boat moored off the rocks, keeping in the shadows of the moon wherever possible. As they approached the boat they could see it was piled high with pieces of wood from old ships that had come to rest in the port.

"What is the wood for?" Sam asked.

"All in good time". Mawgan replied as they all clambered on board, and the men rowed hell for leather back to the ship.

"Just hoist one sale". Mawgan ordered as three of the crew weighed anchor.

They sailed out until they were only just visible from the shore line. "Man the canons". Mawgan ordered.

"Why" Sam asked in amassment he could see no foe.

"Just do what I say, take the name HMS Action of the ship and fix it to one of the pieces of wood". Mawgan pointed to the wood that was still in the rowing boats they were now towing.

Mawgan got the crew together. "I want the ship to tack and turn so that in the shadow of the moon it will give the impression of two ships. And as we tack I want the canons fired with extra powder to give off a lot of smoke". Mawgan had a cunning plan.

The ship was soon turning this way and that every time they turned five canons would fire, this went on for about ten minutes. Mawgan took the piece of wood that Sam had fixed the name too and threw it over board. He then untied the boats laden with wood and watched them drift away. "Aim the canons on the rowboats". He ordered.

The canons all turned and pointed at the boats which were now bobbing up and down about twenty yards from the ship. "Fire". Came the order.

All the canons fired almost at the same time the noise was deafening the cannon balls hit the water with such force the ship rocked from side to side as if hit by a tidal wave. The little rowing boats were blasted to smithereens.

"Hoist the main sail and let's get out of here". Mawgan shouted as if mission was accomplished.

Mawgan new that all the cannon fire would have been heard on shore and someone would soon sail out to see what was happening and with a bit of luck they would find the ships name and all the wood and think she had sunk.

"Next stop Cornwall". Mawgan shouted as he reached for his razor to shave off his beard and head to remove the red dye.

Chapter 21

Back in Cornwall Willy was making a good recovery but not letting on how good as he was quite enjoying his time at Lowenna's. Lowenna wouldn't let any of her girls bath him she did it herself every night.

Damaris Penrose had ridden down to see Tamasine. She needed to tell her that her Father had taken all of Henrys money she had no money for the children.

"How could he do that it was your husband's money". Tamasine new the man was devious but thought it imposable for him to do that.

"He is a law onto himself he told Henrys lawyer he was investing it for me so the lawyer paid it to him". Damaris was upset.

"Why couldn't you tell the lawyer that you wanted the money?" Tamasine thought that would be easy.

"You met my father no one argues with him no matter who ever you are". Damaris knelt down beside Arthur and Amy. "It's these dears I feel for". She said putting her arms around them.

"They won't miss the money; it's their mother they miss. They have a home here and we will all do what we can for them, but no one can replace their mother". Tamasine also knelt down beside them.

Damaris looked at Tamasine as she put her arm around the children. "Can I stay here" She asked.

"What with us?" Tamasine asked with some surprise.

"I won't ever go back to Bodmin, I hate my Father". Damaris sat on the floor and pulled Amy on to her lap.

"Of course you can stay, do you think your father will come looking for you?" Tamasine also sat on the floor and put her arm around her.

"He's not worried about me now Henry's dead, all he wanted me for was to bear a grandson to inherit his bloody empire". Damaris cuddled Amy in close to her as if she was given the love she would have liked to have felt.

"Have you no brothers to inherit?" Tamasine asked as she tickled Amy under her chin.

"No my mother died when I was young, my father had many women but none boar him a child". Damaris looked as if she had some satisfaction that her Father hadn't fathered a son.

"So why is he so against Sam he could father a child with you"? Tamasine thought that would be so easy.

"He has not got good enough breeding for my father. Unless they have money or land my father conceders them as peasants and no way would he want me to breed from a peasant. The thought of someone bread from a peasant getting hands on his money frightens him to death". Damaris had a tear in her eye her love for Sam was clear to see.

"I wish he would frighten his self to death". Tamasine said as she put her arm around Damaris and gave her a little hug. This put a little smile on Damaris face.

Damaris settled in with Tamasine and the children at Mawgan's cottage, Willy was still staying down at Lowenna's but came up every day to do his choirs and mind his pigs. Rajah still slept in with the contraband and only came out when it was safe to do so.

Three weeks had passed since Damaris arrival. Tamasine and Damaris were out in the garden with the children when they were startled by a group of horse and riders arriving outside the gate. One of the riders pushed forward from the pack it was Lord Tremeldon Damaris's Father. "I thought we would find you here, now get your horse and get home." He raged.

"I'm never coming home this is my home now". Damaris replied quite calmly.

"You will come home with me know". Lord Tremeldon said sternly as he dismounted his horse.

"I will not". Damaris replied angrily.

"You will come home until you give birth to a son of good breading, then you can do what the hell you like". Lord Tremeldon grabbed Damaris by the hair and dragged her towards his horse.

Damaris started kicking him hard in the shins so hard that he let go of her hair. Tremeldon shouted to two of the men. "Get hold of her". He shouted. "I'll show you and these people what happens to people that disobey me". He grabbed a horse whip from the saddle of his horse pulled at the back of Damaris's dress until some flesh was exposed. He stood back and brought the whip down hard on her flesh.

"No no!!!" Little Arthur shouted. He ran over and caught hold of Tremeldon by the leg and started tugging at it. Tremeldon brought the whip down on the boys face. He let go and fell to the ground his hand clutching his face as he fell. Tremeldon bent down and pulled him to his feet. He shouted to another man. "Take him he can go down the mines for his sins". He chuckled as he picked the whip up again and raised it in the air to bring back down on Damaris.

Tamasine had gone into the cottage and returned with the pistols one in each hand. "Bring that whip down again and I will put this between your eyes". She said as she calmly pulled the hammers back.

"You wouldn't dare". Tremeldon replied.

A voice from a man on one of the horses said. "She would he put his hand up to his ear". It was the man that Tamasine had shot when they came looking for Rajah.

"Let her go". Tremeldon ordered to the two men holding her. She ran over to Tamasine and stood beside her.

Tamasine pointed both pistols at the man holding Arthur. "You now!! Let the boy go". She demanded.

"Let him go". Lord Tremeldon said as he mounted his horse and turned it to face Tamasine and Damaris. "Don't think this is the end of it". He said then turned his horse and they all galloped up the lane.

"He won't let that go he'll be back." Damaris sighed. "I have put you all in danger I should never have come down here".

"Nonsense if danger is what it takes for standing up to people like that then bring it on I say". Tamasine gave a nervous laugh as she was shaking with temper and a little fear.

"I wonder who he thinks I'm going to have a son with. I would love to give him a son with Samuel but that's not good enough for him". Damaris bent down and picked up Arthur who was still holding his face. "You are a brave young man". She said as she took a hanky from her pocket, and dipped it in a bucket of cold water that was beside the gate and gently patted his face with it.

"He certainly is." Tamasine said as she put the pistols down on the table in the garden and bent down and picked up Amy "Tell me has your Father always been violent to you".

Damaris pulled up her dress exposing the top of her legs which had a number of scars running across them. "Does that answer your Question"?

"O gosh what a brut." Tamasine looked so sorry for her.

"To be honest the mental torture was worse than the physical pain".

"You poor thing. You said your father had many women but what of your Mother". Tamasine put Amy on the hammock.

"I'm not sure how old I was when my mother died I do remember hiding when he was hitting her. No one has ever told me how she died or what of, but I am convinced he had something to do with it". Damaris put Arthur on the hammock beside Amy.

"I don't know how that man could call himself a father". Tamasine pushed the hammock back and forward.

"I should have stood up to him years ago. If only I had the courage to go away with Samuel things might have been so different. These poor dears mother would still be alive. I've just been a coward and its cost people's lives". Damaris pushed the hammock in turn with Tamasine.

"Don't blame yourself there is only one person to blame and we all know who that is. So come on we are all here for you know". Tamasine put her arm around Damaris.

Chapter 22

A couple of months had passed no one had come looking for Damaris everyone hoped her father had given up on her. Little did they know that Lord Tremeldon and Sir Fredric Stowman where making plans to amalgamate there land and businesses. That is if Sir Fredric's son was to marry Damaris, Lord Tremeldon's daughter and produce an heir. This proposition had not yet been put to Albert Stowman but both parties knew he would go along with it.

Mean while every time Tamasine saw James she kept talking about the Carters and how he never looked at them. Rajah still kept out of his way.

Up at Winnie's James had just arrived back from Penzance looking rather fall awn Winnie could see right away that something was wrong. "What is it"? She asked.

"I have today disobeyed my orders; I have spent the day watching the Carters. It would appear that they are rogues of the top order. Tamasine was right I think it is people like that we should be targeting". James lent forward and kissed Winnie on the forehead.

"What are you going to do"? Winnie put her arms around him.

"I don't know it seems that they store a lot of contraband on what you call the Mount, this is outside my authority but they did come in to Penzance so I will have to think about it". He sighed.

"Now you know that, does it mean you won't bother the local folk". Winnie had gone to the fire were she stirred a pot of stew.

"I will still bother anybody that smuggles no matter how little. As I have said many times they are defrauding King and country. And I cannot stand by and watch".

Winnie dished out a large bowl of stew and took it over to James. "So what you going to do about the Carters"? She asked.

"I am going to watch them and if I find a way to impound there ill gotten gains then I will whatever my orders are". James said quite firmly.

"Good for you, I'm so proud you will really show people around here that you will stand up to your employers when you think something is right."Winnie bent down and gave him a kiss nearly knocking the stew out of his hands.

"I have always believed that everyone should pay their dues no matter who ever they are and whatever the circumstances". James replied doing a balancing act with his stew.

"O well, it will interesting to see what happens if ever you manage to catch them". Winnie said as she went back to the pot and filled a dish for herself.

The next morning James was out early he was going to walk along the coast path to work. He wanted to know if the Carters where selling to one of his employers .If Samuel Hocking was buying he was determined he would expose him. He sat on a rock on the beach for some time there were a lot of small boats coming in and out of the harbour at Pursha cove and on the mount. Just along the beach he noticed a young woman also watching the mount. He decided to go over and introduce himself and see if he could find out what she was up to. "Good morning I'm James Wilmot Sparrow".

"I know who you are." The woman replied as she stood up and started to walk away.

James walked beside her. "I hope you will forgive me for asking, but you seemed to be taking a lot of interest in the boats going in and out of the harbour.

"So what". Came a snappy reply.

"O!! I just wondered if you had any interest in them". James now had to quicken his pace to keep up with the woman.

The woman stopped and quickly turned towards James and pulled a long knife from a sheath which was attached to a belt around her waist. She brandished the knife just inches from his face. "Keep your noise out of our business." She said in a threatening way.

"Ok Ok I was just trying to be friendly". James held his arms out as he said it.

"I don't need friends so I suggest you leave now, unless you want your face altered." The woman still had the knife inches from James's face.

"Ok I'm going I'm going". James replied quite nervously.

James left the woman but had only gone about fifty yards when he met Henri the artist who had seen everything that went on. "You meet Miss Carter then". He laughed as James approached.

"Is that who she is". James now understood why she reacted to him in the way she did. "Tell me what you know of her and her family".

"Henri knows plenty but it stays up here". Henri pointed to his head.

"I need to know if they are as notorious as people say they are". James wanted answers.

"All I will say is you best leave alone. Some people's businesses are best left to them that are doing the business." Henri had a smile on his face.

"There is business and there is robbery". James said firmly.

"O I don't think the Carters would rob anybody". Henri laughed.

"What about King and country not paying your dues that's robbery". James was looking very official.

"I don't think folk round here see it quite like that, now if you excuse me I have a little drawing to complete". Henri turned and climbed up onto the rock.

James left and went on in to Penzance where he met up with his men in the customs house. He explained to them that to-day they were going to target the Carters.

"I don't think that wise." Said the man they call Slaughterhouse.

"Why not." James asked firmly.

"Because there are certain people that won't like it". Slaughterhouse replied.

"I don't care; if they are avoiding duty then we should make sure it stops". James sat down on a chair by a desk full of papers.

"Me and the rest of the men will take no part in it, we will return to Plymouth to-day". Slaughterhouse turned towards the door.

"Why what are you afraid of". James stood up.

130

Slaughterhouse turned and walked back to James he lifted him in the air by the scruff of his neck and shouted. "Afraid what do you mean afraid, I'm afraid of no man, but I won't sever the hand that feeds me". James was shaking with fear but this would not stop him from doing what he thought right. Slaughterhouse dropped James down on a chair in the customs house then left and went out to where the other men where holding their horses. "Come on where off". He said taking his horse mounting up and galloping off with the others following. James was now left alone his protectors had gone but he was determined not to let that deter him from doing what he thought was right. He asked a man that he had questioned before about smuggling if he would row him out to the mount what he was going to do when he got there he was un shore.

Back at Mawgan's Winnie had gone down to see Tamasine she went to tell her that James was going to look into the affairs of the Carters.

"Does that mean he will leave the rest alone"? Tamasine asked.

"No I don't think so, you know how he feels about avoiding duty as he calls it". Winnie went over to the corner of the garden where Arthur was looking out to sea with a telescope. "Can you see anything interesting"? She asked.

"No". Arthur replied. "I look every day to see if Mawgan's coming".

Winnie turned to Tamasine. "He should be back soon."

"I can't wait I miss him so much, I pray each night they are all fine". Tamasine sighed.

Winnie stayed down all day with Tamasine and the children. It was around four PM when Winnie said. "I must go now and get James a meal ready for when he gets home".

"That sounds like a woman in love, when you look after a man's stomach". Tamasine said in a teasing way.

"I didn't think I would ever admit it and I know you all think him weird, but I do love him I just can't imagine him not being here". Winnie had never talked like that about any man before.

Tamasine put her arm around her. "I'm so glad for you." She replied, thinking at least Mawgan won't go with her now.

Winnie left and went back to her cottage to cook James a meal. The meal was ready and Winnie kept looking at the clock and the door as James was now quite late. She went out the gate and up the lane a little way but no sign of him. As the time went on Winnie got more and more anxious. It had now got to seven thirty and he still wasn't home so she decided to go down and see Tamasine as she didn't really know what to do.

Tamasine said. "I expect there's a perfect explanation he is probably held up with some smuggler or other."

"He's never been late like this I'm sure something has happened to him. Will you come to Penzance with me to see if we can find him"? She asked.

"It's a bit late to go in there and besides I have the children to care for."Tamasine replied as she picked up Amy.

"I'll look after them". Damaris said as put a cloth down from wiping some dishes.

"Ok if you don't mind". Tamasine said. If it puts your mind at rest I expect he's fine after all he has that great big oaf to look after him. Best we get Willy to saddle a couple of horses before he goes down to Lowenna's, it will be quicker and safer if we ride in.

Ten minutes later and they were on their way and within the hour were in Penzance harbour riding their horses around drunks and prostitutes.

They arrived at the customs house which was all locked up Tamasine demounted from her horse and went over to an old man with a gray beard he was sitting on a capstan smoking a clay pipe. Tamasine had seen him before with Mawgan.

"Youm Mawgans maid in E!!"? He Asked.

"You could say that I suppose". She replied. "Now tell me have you seen anyone at the customs house to-day."

"The all skitadlled this morning, the big bugger E was real mad e was".

"What you mean they left". Winnie said surprisingly.

"Yeh and they en coming back i'd say". The man sucked on his pipe and chuckled.

"What makes you say that"? Tamasine asked as she held her horse.

The man just laughed.

"Tell me did they all go". Winnie couldn't believe James would leave without telling her.

"Na not the posh bugger E diden go".

"Who do you mean James"? Winnie's face lit up.

"Is that what e's called posh bugger us calls im, E went off in a boat with old Roger over there". The man pointed to a man mending nets further over on the quay.

"Thank you". Winnie said, Tamasine and her led their horses over to the man.

"Hello". Winnie said. "I believe you took James the revenue man out in your boat today".

The man just nodded nervously.

"Can you tell us where he is now"? Winnie thought this is going to be hard work as the man just shrugged his shoulders.

Tamasine then tried. "It is very important that we find him". The man just shrugged his shoulders again.

She then had a thought knowing how well Mawgan was respected she thought she would use his name. "Look I do need to find him before Mawgan returns".

"I left him on the Mount". The man blurted out.

"Are you going back to fetch him"? Winnie asked.

"Not bloody likely." The man said as he stood up.

"Why not". Winnie looked surprised as she said it.

"I'll leave him to the Carters I'm not going back". The man was sure of that.

"What are we going to do now?" Winnie turned to Tamasine and asked.

"I'm not sure, we could always go back and get a boat and go and get him I suppose". Tamasine thought it was a bit of a mad brain idea. But she knew it was something Mawgan would do especially where Winnie was concerned.

"Come on then let's go" Winnie said with some excitement.

It was now around midnight when they got back to Mawgan's cottage. "Have you found him?" Damaris asked anxiously as they opened the door.

"No but we know where he is, and we are going to get him". Winnie said as Tamasine went and checked on the children.

"I been thinking, I don't think It's such a good idea me and you going on our own". Tamasine now wanted to get out of it.

"Come on it was your idea; if it was Mawgan you would have no hesitation in going". Winnie wasn't going to let her back out now.

"I'll go with you". Rajah said as he appeared from the chimney and went over and shut the door that had been left open.

"Will you". Winnie now thought they would be off.

"Now hang on". Tamasine said. "James is still supposed to be looking for Rajah what's going to happen if he turns up".

"I forgot that, you hadn't better come". Winnie flopped down in the chair in disappointment.

"If only Mawgan was here". Tamasine sighed then looked at Winnie. "Come on girl lets go. That's if you're all right with the children Damaris". She asked.

"Yes I'm fine, but you pair be careful mind". Damaris thought they were being really brave.

The pear of them went down on the quay and pushed a small rowing boat out in the water. They rowed there way over to St Michel's Mount. They moored up on some rocks a little way from the quay. As they quietly crept up the rocks towards the buildings on the quay they could see fires flickering and could hear men talking.

"You would think these buggers would be in bed". Winnie whispered.

As they looked down on the quay from their advantage point Tamasine accidently kicked a stone that rolled down and made what seemed to be a loud noise. A man with a rifle looked up pointing the rifle towards were they were. He looked there for a couple of minutes before turning and going back to one of the fires.

"I thought you were going to die a virgin then". Winnie was shaking as she said it to Tamasine.

"I couldn't say that about you". Tamasine replied.

They decided if they went a little further along they could get down a little closer to the buildings. As they were getting closer they suddenly stopped as a ship moored on the key had lanterns that seemed to be being lit all at the same time. A man left the ship and shouted. "Come on the tides right to go".

"That's Harry Carter he is a Captain." Tamasine whispered.

"What do you think they are up to"? Winnie asked.

"They have obviously been waiting for the tide too sail". Tamasine replied.

About twenty men appeared and started to make their way down to the ship. One man appeared from a building with James, whose hands were tied together with a piece of rope coming from them which the man was pulling. "What shall I do with him"? The man shouted holding the rope in the air.

"Lock him in here". One of the others shouted back as he opened a small door on the end of the quay.

The man pulling James by the rope shoved him in the door and bolted it from the outside. He then continued on down to the ship.

Tamasine and Winnie waited there for what seemed ages before the ship left. As soon as it had gone Winnie was all for running down and letting James out.

"Hang on". Tamasine insisted. "Let's just make sure they have all gone, as you said before I don't want to end up a dead virgin".

"Live or die I believe you will always be a virgin". Winnie giggled.

After about ten minutes they nervously crept down to where James was locked in. Winnie slowly slid the bolt back but in the dead of night it made a loud screeching sound. "Quietly!!" Tamasine whispered nervously looking all around.

The door opened and James appeared his hands still tied. "What the hell are you two doing here"? He said looking rather surprised.

"That's a nice greeting; I thought you would be glad to see us". Winnie replied as she tugged at the knots on the rope trying to undo them.

"O believe me I am". James replied as he was pulling his hands as Winnie was pulling the knots.

With James freed they made their way to the rowing boat and rowed back to Mawgan's quay and walked up to his cottage. It was now breaking daylight and Damaris was waiting for them she hadn't gone to bed.

They sat down around a table. No one had spoken since they left the Mount.

"How did they treat you, were you frightened, you're lucky they didn't kill you"? Winnie was asking question after question.

"Woo, woo, slow down a little". James replied. "They were not going to kill me, in fact I was surprised. One of the Carter brothers spent a long time talking to me. They don't see their self's as criminals they see their self's as honest business men who work hard for their money".

"But that's what they are business men". Tamasine said as she took a kettle of the fire and toped up the tea pot.

"If they avoid paying duty then they are criminals". James stressed.

"Let's not argue about it, let's just be thankful James is all right". Winnie stood up and put her arms around him.

"I still don't think them as criminals, like James said they didn't hurt him, they didn't hide their business, I think criminals are people that hurt people, and take things that don't belong to them. I know what Mawgan would say, people like Damaris father are criminals and they get away with it. There's no one on his back." Tamasine said quite forcefully.

"Do you know I agree with you in some instances, but one man's wrong doesn't make another man's wrong right". James pated Winnie on her hand that was resting on his shoulder.

"That's the sort of thing Lily-Rose would say, now come on let's get home and get a couple of hours sleep". Winnie put her hand down for James to catch hold of so she could pull on it to get him moving.

They all said there good bye's and James and Winnie left. Damaris went on to bed for a couple of hours. Tamasine sat down in a large arm chair and shut her eyes and was soon fast asleep.

Chapter 23

Only a couple of hours had past until the children were out of bed. Arthur seeing Tamasine asleep took Amy outside it was a beautiful morning the sun shining. They hadn't been outside long before Arthur came running back in; he shook Tamasine to wake her up. "Come quickly". He shouted full of excitement.

"Whatever is it? Tamasine asked as she got up from the chair rubbing her eyes and following Arthur outside.

Arthur picked up the telescope that he had put down on the hammock and handed it to her. "Look look". He shouted.

Tamasine put the telescope to her eye and looked out to sea scanning right to left. Then she saw it the Cornish flag flying proud on the main mast of a ship. She dropped the telescope on the hammock and turned to Arthur and lifted him high in the air and spun him around and around shouting. "Mawgan's home, he's home he's home, he's home".

With all the commotion they were soon joined by Rajah and Willy. They two were full of excitement when they knew what was going on.

It took a couple of hours before the ship got in and dock. All the people in the area where down on the quay to welcome Mawgan home.

As soon as they had tied up alongside and disembarked from the ship Mawgan made a bee line for Tamasine and flung his arms around her. "God I've missed you". He said as he squeezed her tight.

Rajah was jumping with excitement as Annabel emerged on to the gang plank and started to disembark, she jumped of the end of the plank in to Rajah's arms who swung her around and around. His enjoyment of seeing her was clear for all to see. There was no doubting the love that was there.

Mawgan let Tamasine go. "Now tell me what's happened whilst I've been away".

"O nothing much". Tamasine replied with a smile.

Tamasine suddenly noticed the Indian girl beside the ship. "Who's that"? She asked wondering what Mawgan had been up to.

Mawgan beckoned her over. "Mala I would like you to meet my girl Tamasine". Mala held her hand out and she and Tamasine shook hands.

"Tell me why you are here"? Tamasine asked as she eyed her up and down.

"It's quite simple really she helped Annabel to escape and if she stayed behind in all probability she would have been killed". Mawgan seemed rather pleased with his new acquaintance.

Mala went over to Annabel and Rajah, Tamasine was still eyeing her up and down. "I bet you couldn't keep your hands off her on your voyage". She said to Mawgan.

"I can honestly say I have been celibate the whole voyage even though she did tell me she does a good gig a gig". Mawgan wanted to assure her that he had changed and he did just want her.

Willy came over to Mawgan. "What cargo us got *Cap 'n*". He asked

"We got plenty of precious things". Mawgan replied. "We'll unload her tomorrow".

"Can *E* wait *Cap 'n*". Willy replied full of enthusiasm.

Mawgan carried Amy up the hill to his cottage he had missed the children. Arthur kept asking questions about the voyage. Winnie had come down on the Quay but not James. He said best he didn't see what goods Mawgan had brought back with him. He thought he owed Tamasine that much.

When they got up to the cottage Rajah said he would make everyone a cup of tea and bring it out to the garden. Arthur ran over and picked up the telescope and brought it over to Mawgan. "I saw you first". He said.

"Did you now" Mawgan replied as he picked him up and sat him on his knee. He then turned to Damaris. "Now tell me how we are blessed with your presence".

Damaris told him all about her father and what had happened.

It took the rest of the morning for them all to tell everything that had happened.

Mawgan asked Willy to go down on the ship and bring up a parcel that was in his cabin.

Willy was gone for about half an hour when he returned he had a parcel under his arm and a sack over his shoulder. "Can I *ave* some of this *backe Cap'n?*".He asked as he handed Mawgan the parcel and dropped the sack on the ground.

Mawgan roared with laughter. "You can try and smoke it but it's not backe".

"What is it *Cap'n*". Willy now had his hand in the sack and brought out a handful of the red and yellow strands.

"They tell me what you are handling is worth more than gold in are city's". Mawgan took a handful for Tamasine to smell.

"It's certainly not a perfume". Tamasine replied turning up her nose as she did so.

"It's saffron". Rajah said as he to smelt it.

"What do *E* do with it". Willy was still disappointed it wasn't tobacco.

"You cook with it". Rajah still had his arm around Annabel they both laughed as Rajah replied.

"You better take a hand full down to old Mother Cory she's always cooking something special". Mawgan put a hand full in some paper that was on the table he pulled all the ends up and twisted the top and handed it to Willy.

"Never mind all that, what's in the parcel"? Tamasine wasn't very excited about the saffron.

"This my dear is for you". Mawgan undone the string that was holding it together and past the parcel still wrapped to Tamasine.

She quickly had the wrapping off like and excited chid. Inside was the most beautiful silk that royalty would be proud to wear. Tamasine held it up against herself. "O it's beautiful". She said as she went over and gave Mawgan a kiss.

Mawgan asked if everyone could be down on the quay at five the next morning as he wanted to unload the ship and it would take quite some time.

"Now you are back me and the children will go home tonight". Tamasine said still holding the silk close to her. "O and what about Mala does she want to stay with me".

"She'll be fine here". Mawgan replied.

"I knew it you want her in your bed". Tamasine said angrily.

Mawgan laughed. "I don't want her in my bed, if I did I had plenty of opportunity I made you a promise when I left. It might have been difficult but I have kept that promise". Mawgan lifted up Amy and passed her to Tamasine kissed her on the cheek then said. "I only thought it better she stays with Annabel for the moment".

Tamasine smiled and kissed him back. "Thank you for my present". She whispered she knew if Mawgan said he hadn't then he hadn't.

Everyone had an early night that night excited about the unloading of Mawgan's ship. Knowing what ever was on the ship they would all benefit from it.

At five AM dawn was just braking with a beautiful red sky there must have been around fifty people down on the quay waiting to help.

Mawgan and the crew soon had the hold of the ship opened up and people were carrying sacks and bundles in to a warehouse.

With the ship half empty Mawgan declared it's time for a break they all sat around the quay. Tamasine had a metal tea pot so big she could hardly lift it she was walking amongst the people pouring out tea. Suddenly there was shout. "I haven't got enough for everyone". It was Mother Cory she had a large try full of buns that by the smell alone said they had just come out of the oven.

Mother Cory walked amongst the people handing out the buns starting with Mawgan. You could see by the way people reacted that they had tasted nothing like it before. "What kind of buns are they". One of the people asked.

"I don't know". Mother Cory turned to Mawgan. "What was that stuff Willy brought me down called"? She asked.

"Saffron". Mawgan shouted.

"Then I suppose they are saffron buns". Mother Cory replied with tone of delight as like most cooks the enjoyment is seeing others enjoy what you have made brought her most pleasure.

With the break over the continuing of unloading the ship began with the talk of the saffron buns ringing around. It was clear to Mawgan that his saffron would not reach the big city's it would never leave Cornwall.

The last lot of cargo had been unloaded and every one had their bits. Some had tobacco some had cloths others had alcohol of one sort or another.

Suddenly there was a sound of horses and in a matter of moments the quay was full of riders led by Albert Stoneham. He forced his horse through the people on the quay and went up too Damaris. "I've come to take you home to your father". He said quite emphatically.

Mawgan got in front of her. "And what if she doesn't want to go"? He asked just as emphatically.

"Then we will take her by force". Stoneham replied. He then dismounted his horse and put his hand on Mawgan's shoulder and led him to one side.

Mawgan pushed his hand off. "I thought you a friend". He said.

"You made a big mistake Mawgan when you double-crossed me. I think you owe me some gold". Stoneham even when he was angry looked slimy.

"I owe you nothing I done exactly what was agreed; it's you that have crossed me in more than one way". Mawgan was thinking of what Tamasine had told him and he was finding it hard not to punch the man.

"You agreed to take ore to Spain of which I paid you good money but you failed me".

"No you failed me when we got to Spain there was no one there to meet us".

"But your ship was stopped and searched before you left the bay".

"I had two ships leave the bay, do you think I didn't know what you were up too, now I would be grateful if you and your toy soldiers will leave my quay". Mawgan pointed to the lane leading away from the quay.

"I came here for Damaris and I won't be leaving without her."Stoneham led his horse over to where Tamasine and Damaris were standing. As he approached Tamasine spat on the ground in front of him. "Charming". He said as he pushed her to one side.

"You're coming with me Miss." Stoneham put his hand on Damaris shoulder.

"Get your filthy hand off her". Tamasine shouted as she pushed between the pair of them.

"Don't cross me again or I won't be so lenient this time". Stoneham pushed Tamasine to the floor.

Mawgan ran over and pushed Stoneham causing him to fall over. With Stoneham on the ground Mawgan bent over and helped Tamasine to her feet as he pulled her up Stoneham was also up and had a pistol pointing at Mawgan's head. "Get back out of my way". He shouted as he pulled the hammer back.

"Pull the trigger or get of my quay". Mawgan wasn't going to be frightened by him.

"Were going and taking Damaris with us". Stoneham still had the pistol pointed at Mawgan.

Suddenly there was a shout. "She's going knower". It was Samuel he came charging across putting his arms around Stoneham and they both went to the ground. Samuel was on top of Stoneham there was a loud crack as Stoneham's pistol went off.

Some of Stoneham's men had dismounted and were now over by them one of them pulled Samuel off Stoneham he had blood coming from his stomach. The man just through him to the ground and then helped Stoneham up.

Tamasine and Damaris quickly got down tending to Samuel. "We should get him to Lilly-Rose". Tamasine said as she tore a piece of the bottom of her dress and held it against the wound.

Stoneham made a gesture to his men to draw there pistols. "There is only one person leaving here". He said as he dragged Damaris off Samuel.

"Don't you think you've done enough"? Mawgan said as he squeezed the arm of Stoneham until he let her go.

Two of Stoneham's men grabbed Mawgan and held him tight, he wriggled and fought but they were too strong for him, and they soon had him pinned to the ground.

Two more had Damaris hold she too tried to fight them but to no avail. Another man tied her hands and legs. One through her over his shoulder and put her over a saddle on a horse. Then he tied her hands to her legs under the belly of the horse.

No one tried to stop them as it was clear they would not be able to.

The two men holding Mawgan slowly got him to his feet. Stoneham had mounted his horse and had the regains of the horse that Damaris was on. Mawgan fought no more it was clear he could do nothing. All the men where now on their horses and they started to ride off.

As the past Tamasine who was still on her knees tending to Samuels' wound. Damaris shouted. "Please, please don't let him die".

As soon as they had gone Mawgan said. "Quick let's get him over to Lilly-Rose". He was now down beside Tamasine.

Willy came over. "Perhaps it would be better to take him over to Lowenna, she cured me". He said as he bent down to help carry him.

"I don't think he will react to the same medicine as you did". Mawgan chuckled as the lifted Samuel up and carried him over to Lilly-Rose.

Lilly-Rose said she would have to remove the lead but she was sure he would live.

They left Samuel there knowing he was in good hands "What are we going to do about Damaris"? Tamasine asked Mawgan.

"I'm not sure; think we should sleep on it". Mawgan was sure he would work out something.

Chapter 24

The next morning James went down to Mawgan's. "Mawgan". He said calmly. "Yesterday I turned a blind eye to what I saw. I did so as I thought I owed that much to Miss Tamasine for what she had done in helping Winnie with my rescue. But there are things that are on my conscious and that I can't turn a blind eye to. Rajah for one I feel I should be reporting that he is still here".

"My dear James I don't know what point there would be in reporting him. I remember you telling me that you weren't interested in any fugitive". Mawgan had more on his mind than worrying about what James was going to do.

"That was before I was given the task of capturing him". James pushed his chest out in a proud way.

"That was months ago, the task failed and no one's bothered since". Winnie said angrily she had no idea James was going to mention Rajah.

"And what about Willy and the beating he took, do you want something like that to happen again". Tamasine too was quite angry.

"You know what they say once a government man always a government man. Now I don't want to be rude but we have Damaris to think about". Mawgan was trying to think of a way to get her away from her father.

"I here she is to be married next week". James said as he made meanings to Winnie for them to leave.

Mawgan turned quickly. "What do you mean married". He asked.

"I hear she is to marry Albert Stoneham next week".

"The bastard he wouldn't say no to fathering a child". Tamasine would never forget what he had tried to do to her.

"Look Mawgan I will say nothing about Rajah, but please don't put me in these positions". James held his hand out for Mawgan to shake.

Mawgan shock his hand and said. "Like you I will never stop doing what I think is right".

"I respect you for that". James said as he and Winnie made for the door.

With Winnie and James gone Mawgan asked Tamasine if she wanted to go to Bodmin with him. "It will probably mean sleeping out tonight". He said.

"I'm worried about leaving the children what if they do come looking for Rajah". Tamasine wanted to go but was so worried.

"I don't think that will happen after all they would be safe with Annabel nobody knows who she is". Mawgan so much wanted her along.

"I suppose your right; I'll go and ask her". Tamasine went outside where Annabel was playing with Rajah and the children.

"Willy". Mawgan shouted. "Saddle up a couple of horses".

"I,I, *Cap'n*". Willy replied.

Tamasine returned. "I will have to go and get changed". She said.

"You look lovely as you are". Mawgan replied with a smile.

"A bout time, I thought you had lost your charm". Tamasine kissed him on the cheek as she past him in the door way.

Willy arrived out in the lane with the horses Mawgan tied some blankets to the saddles. "We will go down and see how Samuel is before we leave but I need you to keep an eye on him". Mawgan said to Willy as he patted him on the back.

Mawgan mounted up and rode up to pick up Tamasine the then went down to Lily-Rose who was sitting outside smoking her clay pipe.

"How's the wounded". Mawgan asked as he demounted his horse.

"It'll take a day or two but he'll live". Lilly replied as she got up and stroked the horses.

After a few minutes spent with Samuel Tamasine and Mawgan left and started off to Bodmin.

It was a long hard ride neither one of them had any idea what they were going to do when they got there. They stopped by a ford about five miles away to water the horses and give them a bit of a rest. "We should have brought an extra horse for Damaris". Tamasine said as she put her arm around her horse's neck and stroked it.

"I was thinking that, but if we find her I don't think we should take her back home with us as it's the first place they'll look". Mawgan had the rains of his horse hold loosely so that the horse could drink from the ford.

"Where can we hide her"? Tamasine asked as she led her horse over by a grass bank and sat on it.

Mawgan led his horse over and sat down beside her. "Let's find her first then we can decide what to do".

"I'm sure you'll think of something". Tamasine kissed Mawgan on the cheek then got up and mounted her horse. "Come on we won't find her here". She said a little excited.

Mawgan mounted up and the rode on to the house were they first saw Damaris. They dismounted from their horses and nervously walked up to the front of the house. Mawgan knocked on the big oak door which had a large brass knocker on it. The knock echoed so much so that it put both Tamasine and Mawgan on edge.

There was no answer the walked around the back looking in all the windows as they did so. It soon became clear that no one was living there.

"What do we do now"? Tamasine was disappointed she wasn't there but deep down she knew it wasn't going to be that easy.

"I expect she's locked away at her father's". Mawgan was looking deep in thought as he had no idea what to do now.

They left the house and led their horses as they walked down the lane and back towards Bodmin centre.

"Do you think if I went up and asked to see her they would let me"? Tamasine could see no other way.

"I don't think that wise". Mawgan paused thought for a moment. "Surely in a house that size full of servants someone must feel sorry for her". He said as they now got close to Bodmin town centre.

"I'm sure of it but how do we find out whom, or get to speak to someone at all. Tamasine said as her horse nodded almost like he was in agreement with her.

"I have an idea, if we went and saw that Mr Richards the farmer he might tell us something. After all he was genially cut up about Victoria the children's mother". Mawgan put one foot in the stirrup ready to mount up.

"We have nothing to lose". Tamasine also had a foot in the stirrup.

They both mounted up and galloped off to farmer Richards. The light was fading now, as the made there way up the track they could see a lantern flickering in one of the sheds. As they approached the shed they dismounted and approached very gingerly.

Mawgan didn't know whether it best to knock on the shed door or just open it and go in. So he done both a little tap then opened the door the same time. "Mr Richards". He shouted as he entered with Tamasine close behind.

The farmer was milking a cow; he jumped feet nearly knocking the bucket of milk over. "Bloody hell, you didn't half give me a fright". He said as he stood up clinging to the bucket making sure not to spill a drop.

"Sorry about that, I couldn't think of another way of letting you know we were here". Mawgan reached out to shake his hand.

"Well what do you want you haven't come all this way for a social visit"? Mr. Richards was abrupt and to the point.

"That's true. Mawgan replied, he then told him all that had happened and how they wanted to help Damaris.

"You pair seem to like playing with fire; you'll end up hung if you aren't careful". The farmer gave a nervous smile.

"I think lord Tremeldon would have done that to us by now if he could". Mawgan gave a little chuckle. "Now can you help us or not"? This sounded more like a plea than question.

"You pair might not worry about being hung, but I'm bloody sure I want to keep my neck". Farmer Richards wasn't going to put his self in danger.

"Look whatever you tell us stays with us, all we want to know is, if you know anyone in the house who is sympathetic towards Damaris and how we can contact them". All Mawgan wanted was a name.

"There is a maid she hasn't said much but I can tell she doesn't like what she sees".

The farmer put the bucket of milk he was holding down.

"How can we find this maid"? Tamasine asked she was now felling quite excited.

"You don't approach her on my land, you stay well away. But she comes here about five thirty every morning for the milk for the house". Mawgan could tell Farmer Richards was nervous by the way he said it.

"We won't we will catch her on route somewhere". Mawgan held his hand out for the farmer to shake. "I can't thank you enough". Mawgan said as they shook hands.

Mawgan and Tamasine left. There priority now was to find somewhere to sleep.

"I think we should get as close to the house as possible to sleep". Tamasine said as the trotted down the lane.

"I agree we passed a little wood nearby, if we tethered the horses out of site in there then we will have to find a nice field to sleep in". Mawgan was looking forward to spend the night with Tamasine. He thought sleeping under the stars added something to it.

"I think you are a bit of romantic on the quite". Tamasine could almost read his thoughts.

They soon got to the woods and made their way in to them until they came to a little grass patch it had a stream running through it. "This is just fine". Mawgan said. He removed the saddles from the horses took a rope from the back of his saddle and tied it between two trees, then tethered the horse's to the rope so they could walk up and down to the grass and stream or even lie down. "That's them comfortable; I think we should spend the night here with the horses". Mawgan gave a little wink.

"I've been wondering how we will know which way she will walk to the farm". Tamasine thought there must be a closer way than the way they had come

"Good point I think we should investigate up around the house to-night, just to see if there are any paths leading towards the farm". Mawgan thought what fools not to ask the farmer which way she comes.

They left the horses and walked on until they came to the long gravelled drive leading to Fawn House. As soon as they put their feet on the gravel it made a loud crunching sound. The quickly got on the grass beside the drive and gingerly walked up towards the house. As they got closer to the house they could see glimmers of light which looked like carriage lamps. Mawgan beckoned to Tamasine to duck down and crawl the rest of the way. When they got to the house there was a small wall between the grass and the gravel. They lay on the grass behind it just peering over the top. There were two carriages on the gravel close to the house. Both had a candle light on each corner they also had a horse man and a footman with them; it was obvious they belonged to some one of importance. "Who do you think they belong to"? Tamasine whispered.

"No Idea". Mawgan replied in a whisper as he pulled Tamasine down as she had her head up way above the wall.

Suddenly there was a light at the door and a group of people appeared. "It's that slime ball Stoneham". Tamasine shrieked as Mawgan again had to pull her down.

"That's his father Sir Frederick with him". Mawgan said as Sir Frederick and his son got into the first carriage.

Then three other people came out and got in the second carriage. "Who's that"? Tamasine was now lying flat on the grass with her head peeping over the wall.

"I've no Idea". Mawgan replied as he lied down beside her.

The carriages left and made their way down the gravel drive.

Mawgan and Tamasine waited a few minutes, their hearts beating with excitement and fear. Then they were alerted by another light which soon became clear it was a girl of about eighteen carrying a lantern and walking nervously across the grass at the side of the house. "I wonder what she's up to". Tamasine said as she stood up as now there was no one in the courtyard.

"There's one way to find out". Mawgan stood up beside her and beckoned for her to follow him.

As they tiptoed across the gravel to get to the side of the house were the girl came out of. It crunched under their feet which to them seemed quit loud. They went down across the grass following the girl she had a lantern in one hand and now they could see she was carrying a basket. When they got down to where the grass ended there was a kissing gate that led into the wood. Mawgan and Tamasine where now only a few yards behind the girl as she went through the gate. She nervously looked around like she was checking she wasn't being followed. Mawgan and Tamasine dropped to the ground so not to be seen.

"Look". Mawgan whispered there under a large tree was a young boy of around six or seven. He too was carrying a basket.

When the girl approached him they exchanged baskets.

Mawgan could see what was going on so he decided to approach the girl. "What's going on here"? He said quit bluntly.

The girl jumped feet. "Nothing sir". She replied nervously putting the basket behind her back as if to hide it.

"I would say you are stealing from your employer". Mawgan replied as he looked into the basket the boy was now carrying.

"Please sir don't tell his Lordship he will have me whipped". The girl was now shaking.

The boy stood up tall. "Don't blame her Sir I asked her for it".

"Did you and what do you need it for". Mawgan could see in the boys eyes there was a good reason behind it.

"It's for his Mother, my ant she is very poorly and week. Her husband died in a cart accident he worked for his Lordship and when he died his Lordship had them evicted from their cottage". The girl showed no emotion but was shaking nervously.

Tamasine thought how strong she was and put her arm around her. "No one is going to tell his Lordship". She said trying to reassure the girl.

Mawgan knelt down beside the boy. "Where do you live now"? He asked.

The boy pointed to some old ships sails that were up against a hedge about thirty yards away.

"I have to go back". The girl said nervously.

"Of course but before you go do you know his Lordships daughter". Mawgan new she mustn't get caught but he thought this the time to find out more.

"She's locked in her room she has a man guarding her". The girl kept looking around to see if anyone was looking for her.

"We want to rescue her, and we need to know how we can get to her". Tamasine still had her arm around her.

"Are you captain Mawgan"? The girl suddenly asked.

"I might be why". Mawgan replied.

"I heard his Lordship talking to Sir Fredrick he said you are going to hang". The girl now looked even more nervous".

"I don't think that likely do you". Mawgan laughed.

"I don't know sir but they were pretty adamant". The girl started to shake again.

Tamasine hugged her "Don't worry about Mawgan he's too smart for them. Now tell us how we can rescue Damaris". Tamasine wanted not to keep her much longer she was beginning to worry for her safety.

"I don't all I can say is everyone will be away tomorrow. They will be away for two days. All that is except cook me and another made". The girl paused then suddenly continued. "O and of course Damaris and her guard Mr Slaughterhouse".

"Thank you now you better run on, we have till tomorrow to think of a way to get Slaughterhouse out of the way". Mawgan pated the girl on her shoulder as he said it.

"Tell me are you the girl that goes for the milk in the morning". Tamasine asked as the girl started to leave.

"Yes Miss I go down this path at five O' clock". The girl left and ran back up across the grass.

Mawgan turned to the boy. "Now then let's see where you live". He said.

The boy led them over to where the sale cloth was up across a couple of post leaning against the hedge. The boy crawled in a narrow entrance Mawgan and Tamasine followed it was very cramped in the back lying with her feet towards the hedge was a women in her thirty's she could not be more than five stone.

"I've never seen anyone so thin". Tamasine whispered to Mawgan.

"No she is obviously not eating". Mawgan replied.

The woman found it hard to speak. But in a very husky voice which was no louder than a whisper she asked. "Will you take my boy and look after him. I have no money or food. I can't stand on my legs".

"No wonder you are cold wet and hungry, you can't live like this". Tamasine said as she knelt down beside her.

"We can't leave her here". Mawgan knew he couldn't walk away and leave someone like this. But he didn't know what to do.

"Can't we take them with us"? Tamasine asked.

"How we only have two horses no carriage or trap, and besides she is not well enough to travel". Mawgan was being realistic.

"We could spend the night and make the place more homely and water tight". Tamasine insisted.

"I think that's the most we can do at the moment". Mawgan replied he put his hand in his pocket and took out two gold coins and handed them to the boy. "Tomorrow you must get some food for your mother".

"Thank you sir". The boy replied as he looked down at his mother.

Chapter 25

They worked all night fetching poles and rebuilding what could only be described as a hovel but it was far better than what was there before. They made it wigwam style so that they could have a fire in the middle.

It was just before five AM when the girl they met last night came by. "Have you done this"? She asked looking amassed at what they had done with the wigwam.

"We would like to have done more". Mawgan replied looking pleased at what they had achieved.

"I will collect some magic mushrooms and put them in Mr Slaughterhouse's breakfast that should make him bad; it might give you the chance you want". The girl said as she went inside the wigwam to see her aunt.

"Won't that kill him"? Tamasine didn't want that on her conscious even though she had heard what a thug he was.

"If I get it right he will just be delirious and have severe stomach ache". The girl thought it a bit funny as she imagined this big man in pain.

"It's worth a try". Mawgan replied. "Now tell me what time is his lordship and party leaving.

"Nine O' clock sir".

Before the girl left Mawgan told her of a plan he had and asked her to go along with it. This she agreed and she told Mawgan which room Damaris was in and which of the keys in the kitchen was to her room.

Just before the girl left to go and get the milk Mawgan pulled some more coins out of his pocket. "I have given the lad some money for food, but please take this and get some help for her". Mawgan gently placed the money in the girl's hand.

"I don't know what to say, is this for real, why would you do this for us, you are so kind". The girl stretched up and kissed Mawgan on the cheek with a tear running down hers, she then ran off towards farmer Richards.

"She's right". Tamasine said. "You are just a wonderful man".

"What you saying any woman that ends up in my bed would be very lucky". Mawgan smiled at her.

"I wouldn't go that far". Tamasine joked.

"What a night, not the night I had planed". Mawgan said as they left the wigwam.

"And what pray did you have planed". Tamasine put her hand in Mawgan's as they made their way back to where they left the horses.

"It was going to start with you lying in my arms and us both looking at the stars". Mawgan gently squeezed her hand.

"Dare I ask how it would have finished"? Tamasine looked up at Mawgan and smiled.

"Let's just say I couldn't see the stars from my position".

They had now reached the horses. Mawgan went over to the stream knelt down, cupped his hands together and dipped them in the water; he brought it up and washed his face.

Tamasine knelt down beside him put her hand in the water and flicked it over Mawgan. This went on for a few minutes with them both flicking water over one another. It led to Tamasine giving Mawgan a passionate kiss. Mawgan gently eased her back so she was lying on her back his hands had just started to explore her body when there was a shout. "I've got the mushrooms". It was the girl returning with the milk.

Mawgan and Tamasine quickly jumped up and laughed at one another. "That's good". Mawgan replied as he quickly walked over to where the shout came from.

The girl showed them the mushrooms and then made her way back up to the house.

Tamasine looked up at Mawgan. "I was saved by the mushroom this time". She said with a smile.

Mawgan wondered would he ever have his Tamasine.

Mawgan and Tamasine brushed the horses down the best they could. Then they eat what little food they had left. They saddled up the horses and led them closer to the edge of the wood where it joined the edge of the grass at the side of the house.

When they got there they could hear a lot of commotion at the front of the house but could not see what was going on. But it soon became clear that it was Lord Tremeldon and his party leaving for Falmouth.

They had left about thirty minutes. Mawgan and Tamasine where getting quite anxious as they made their way up across the grass to the edge of the court yard.   They were wondering what was happening with Slaughterhouse if he had eat the mushrooms.

 After a few minutes the maid appeared. She quickly scampered across the yard to Mawgan and Tamasine. "He ate all the mushrooms, but it has made no effect he is sat outside Damaris door". She said it in such a way that she thought she had let them down.

Mawgan suddenly burst out laughing. "I think it's working now". He said as he pointed to the grass at the front of the house where this big giant of a man was rolling around in agony.

They all turned around and started to laugh. "What now". Tamasine asked Mawgan.

"You go back and stay with the horses and I'll go and get her." Mawgan then turned to the maid. "We have to make this look good". He tied a neck scarf around the bottom of his face as a mask. He then took out a knife from his belt and held it up to the maid. "Ready". He said. They ran across the yard and in the door that led along a passage to the kitchen. He put the knife to the maid's throat as they entered the kitchen where the cook and other maids were. "Just do as I say and no one will get hurt". He said. They both looked quite shaken, in the corner of the kitchen there was a door leading to the pantry. Mawgan led the maid over to the door opened it then indicated to the cook and the maids to get in there. They nervously entered the pantry once they were in Mawgan pushed the girl he was holding in there trying not to hurt her but making it look realistic. He then shut the door and turned the key in the lock.

Mawgan then took the key from where the girl said it was, he then took other keys so that it wouldn't be known that he knew which key to take.

He ran up the stairs to Damaris room unlocked it and burst in. Damaris was sitting on the bed, Mawgan stopped and looked at her he could not believe what he saw she was black and blue there was dry blood around her mouth and nose it was obvious she had taken one hell of a beating.

"I can't go with you". She said as she tried to hide her face.

"Why not, we have come to free you from this". Mawgan sat down beside her.

"Free me I will never be free, my father will hunt me down were ever I go, and what about Sam he could have been killed, and I just know he will be next time, all of you are in danger and I can't live with that". Damaris looked at Mawgan her eyes full of sadness.

"If we don't stand up and do what we think are right people like your father will win every time. Now come with us now. Yes there are risks but we will hide you and Sam some were safe until we decide the best way forward." Mawgan put his arm around her and gave her a reassuring cuddle.

"I won't put you and your people in danger".

Mawgan took his arm from around her turned her face towards his. "Now tell me do you want to be with Sam".

"Off course I do".

"Then please don't worry about me just come with us I know everything will work out in the end".

"I just don't know".

"Well you better come now because when that brut Slaughterhouse comes back I'm dead anyway".

Damaris lent down and picked up a pair of boots and pulled them on. "Well let's go". She said as she stood up.

The crept along the corridor and ran down the stairs through the kitchen and out the door at the back. There was no sign of Slaughterhouse. They were soon down across the grass and in the wood to where Tamasine was with the horses. "What kept you I was beginning to think something had happened"? Tamasine asked as she handed Mawgan the rains of his horse.

"No problems". Mawgan replied as he gave a little wink to Damaris. "Now you will have to get up behind me, we will have to change over a few times to give the horse a rest." Mawgan said as he mounted his horse and then held his arm out to help Damaris to mount.

They made their way out of the woods then at a slow trot they continued on their way. "Have you decided where we can hide her"? Tamasine asked Mawgan.

"Yes no one will surch preacher Jack". Mawgan smiled to himself as he said it.

"Will he take her in"? Tamasine was a little bemused.

"O trust me preacher Jack will do whatever I ask". Mawgan chuckled.

"Best I ask no more". Tamasine replied knowing there was things it was better she didn't know.

Some of the time Damaris was behind Mawgan and then they would change and she would be behind Tamasine. Some of the way they got off and walked the horses to rest them. It was the early hours of the morning before they got home.

The all slept down at Mawgan's and then later that morning Mawgan took Damaris up to preacher Jacks were she was going to stay.

Chapter 26

Four days had now passed since the rescue of Damaris, and it was time to take Sam from Lily-Rose's up to preacher Jacks so he could be with Damaris.

That morning James had told Winnie that he had here'd Lord Tremeldon was coming looking for his daughter and he was going to take Samuel away.

As soon as James had left for work Winnie was down to tell Mawgan.

Mawgan had a plan and he got everybody together. "Willy you go up and see Preacher Jack and tell him the plan goes ahead to-day." He said as he put his hand under his chin and rubbed it.

"I,I!! *Cap'n*" Willy replied and started to go out the door, and then he stopped and turned towards the Captain. "*Do us ave a* plan"? He asked.

"You'll see, to-day we are going to have a funeral, so when you get back hitch up the cart and go over to Billy the wood and pick up a coffin". Mawgan had a slight smile on his face.

"O's dead *Cap'n"?* Willy hadn't heard that anyone had died.

"No one". Mawgan replied.

"Ow can *E ave* a funeral if no one's dead"? Willy was certainly confused.

"You just do as I say and meet us with the coffin down at Lily-Rose's, then it will all come clear". Willy left and Mawgan explained to the rest of them what his plan was. He also told Rajah and Annabel that they should stay hidden all day.

With all that sorted they made their way down to Lily Rose's. It was almost an hour before Willy got there with the coffin. Once there they got the coffin in side they waited to see if Lord Tremeldon arrived as it was paramount to the plan that lord Tremeldon and his men where there when they acted it out .

Sure enough it wasn't long before there was a shout from outside. "Mawgan are you hiding in there." Tremeldon and his men had been up to Mawgan's cottage before making their way towards the quay. Seeing Willy's cart and a crowd gathered outside Lilly-Roses he thought he would find Mawgan there.

Mawgan walked to the door and was confronted by Lord Tremeldon sitting high up on his horse. "Mawgan I'm here on two missions well three actually one to find my daughter two too take into custardy Samuel Rook". He said quite sternly.

"Well sir I can help you with one of your requests ". Mawgan paused and then smiled up at the Lord. "Well that is if you want a body in your custardy, you see we are just about to bury Samuel Rook". Mawgan turned and looked back in the door way and beckoned to them to carry the coffin out. "You haven't said what the third thing is I might be able to help you with that". Mawgan said as Winnie, Willy, Tamasine, with the help of a couple of locals carried the coffin out and placed it on the cart.

"Never mind that now, how did this man die"? Tremeldon asked.

Mawgan looked up at Albert Stoneham who was sat on a horse beside his Lordship. "I should ask your future son in law after all it was he who shot him". Mawgan had a look of anger on his face.

"The bloody fool jumped me". Albert replied quite angrily.

Lord Tremeldon thought he was now going to find his daughter no way would she let Samuel be buried without her being there. He called two of his men forward; he sent one to the church to see if she turned up there, and the other he sent back to Mawgan's house to see if anyone was there hiding.

The funeral position made its way up to the church with Lord Tremeldon and his men following close behind.

Mawgan, Willy, Winnie and Tamasine carried the coffin into the church. The congregation followed along with Tremeldon and his men. "It's good to see such a good turnout". Preacher Jack said sarcastically as he looked at Lord Tremeldon, before giving a short service. The four carried the coffin out to the church yard where it was lowered into the ground.

"When was the grave dug"? Tamasine whispered.

"Yesterday I planned it with Preacher Jack yesterday we didn't know when Tremeldon would be around but we knew he would". Mawgan whispered back felling rather smug.

Once the Preacher had said his few words around the grave they all started to move away when Lord Tremeldon steeped forward. "I'd feel happier if you covered him in before I leave". He said he wanted to be sure he was dead.

Mawgan went over to the pile of earth and picked up two shovels that were lying beside it, he past one to Willy, and he kept the other and in a matter of minutes they had the grave filled in.

As they were shovelling Lord Tremeldon came over and spoke to Mawgan. "If you happen to see the Indian fellow he is no longer a wanted man. You can tell him that the Earls daughter is dead".

"How do you mean dead"? Mawgan tried to sound surprised.

"It would appear that she was kidnapped by some incumbent kidnapers". Lord Tremeldon started to laugh.

"Surely if she was kidnapped she might not be dead". Mawgan knew he had to ask these questions.

"O!! She is the kidnapers had hardly left port when pirates sunk there ship and there was a cannon fight. The kidnaper's ship was sunk and there have been no survivors in fact the ship was blown to smithereens". Lord Tremeldon chuckled he knew Mawgan knew where Rajah was hiding he didn't believe him drowned.

Mawgan smiled to himself he was sure that his rescue of Annabel had fooled everybody, and now he hoped he had fooled them again with the burial of Sam.

What Mawgan didn't know was not only did Lord Tremeldon come looking for his daughter and Samuel he was also in tending to take Mawgan in to custardy and have him tried for treason. He was not giving any hint of this as he wanted to take him in with as little fuss as possible.

They all moved to the edge of the cemetery Lord Tremeldon told two of his men to hide in the cemetery over night he was sure that his daughter would come and visit it.

161

"Mawgan before you go I would like a word with you on your own regarding my third matter". Lord Tremeldon said as if he had something Mawgan might be interested in.

"You go on back I'll be there *drekly"*. Mawgan said to Tamasine and Willy.

They left and made their way back to Mawgan's cottage. When they got there they told Rajah and Annabel all about the funeral and how Rajah was no longer wanted. "How will Samuel survive if he has been buried"? Rajah asked with some concern.

Tamasine laughed. He's not buried he wasn't in the coffin he's still at Lily-Rose's".

She said as she picked up Amy and gave her a cuddle.

Almost an hour had past and Mawgan had not returned to the cottage. Tamasine had started to get a bit anxious.

Rajah said. "Do you think I should go and look for him".

"I don't think that wise". Tamasine replied. "I'll go if he's gone in Winnie's I'll give him what for".

"I expect he's gone down Lily-Rose's to cheek on Samuel". Annabel was trying to reassure every one.

Tamasine left and went first down to Lilly-Rose and then up to the church all that was there were two of Lord Tremeldon's men sitting on the church steps. "The bugger's gone in Winnie's". She whispered to herself as she flumped down the road and banged on Winnie's door.

Winnie answered. "Hi what's up"? She could see Tamasine was troubled.

"Is Mawgan in there"? Tamasine replied sharply.

"No I haven't seen him since the funeral, why!!"

"I'm worried he hasn't returned and something tells me something is wrong". Tamasine had a worried look on her face.

"You know Mawgan he'll turn up *drekly* with his face glowing, some woman I recon". Winnie was trying to reassure Tamasine but was saying the wrong things.

162

Tamasine was about to leave when James came running down the road. He stopped at the gate gasping for breath. "Whatever is it"? Winnie asked as she rushed over to him.

"It's Mawgan". James was finding it hard to get his words out be between his gasp. "He's been taking into custardy charged with treason".

"Whatever do you mean"? Tamasine had such a look of bewilderment on her face.

James had now got his breath back. "Lord Tremeldon and his men have taken him; they are taking him to Truro where he will be tried for treason".

"That's ridiculous, how can they do that". Winnie was now putting her arm around James.

"That bloody Lord Tremeldon thinks he can do anything". Tamasine was now angry.

"Are you sure that's right dear". Winnie asked James.

"O I'm sure he brought him in to me he was in irons. Lord Tremeldon said if his daughter turns up she might be able to save him". James new this was news that no one wanted to hear.

"I wouldn't trust him with that; we must not mention that to Damaris as she would give herself up, we will have to find another way to free him". Tamasine said as she went out the gate and made her way down to Mawgan's cottage to tell the others.

Chapter 27

Over the next couple of days Tamasine had tried to see Mawgan but she was not allowed. James had kept them informed with what was going on and when the trial would start. Tamasine was not over concerned as she was convinced no matter what ever Lord Tremeldon had done no Cornish jury would find Mawgan guilty.

It was now three weeks since Mawgan was taken in to custardy he was taken to a small court just outside Truro and trial was due to start. More people turned up than the little court would hold. Outside was alive with people and carriages. Two carriages arrived the horses looking like they had travailed far and six men got out of each and were quickly ushered in to court.

Winnie had come with Tamasine and they held on to each other as they pushed their way through the crowd and managed to get into the court room. Two men stood up in the front row of the small public gallery and offered them their seats. .

After waiting some time a man down in front of the court stood up and said. "Please be upstanding for his Lordship judge Lord Josiah Tremeldon". Every one stood up as he entered the room.

"I don't believe it why him". Tamasine whispered as they all sat down.

"Bring in the prisoner." The Judge ordered.

Mawgan appeared in irons around his wrists. "O my god what have they done to him". Tamasine sighed as it was clear he had been beaten.

The man that had announced the judge's entrance stood up and read out the charge of treason to Mawgan and asked how he pleaded.

"Not guilty". Came a loud reply.

The judge then said. In normal circumstances we would swear in the jury. But as we have had to go outside to get a jury as people think you as some sort of god in this place. The swearing of the jury has already been done so would you please ask them to take their places."

164

In walked the twelve men that had arrived by coach. "This can't be right". Tamasine stood up and shouted out.

"You be quite". The judge said sternly.

Winnie pulled Tamasine down in her seat.

Mawgan had no legal team to defend him as whoever he had they would not cross Lord Tremeldon. This was just dismissed by the judge but was totally out of order. A man that was the prosecutor stood up and addressed Mawgan. "You are charged with treason it is alleged that you stole iron ore from a local mine and sold it along with a ship to an enemy of our country. Have you anything to say to the charges".

"If you have evidence that supports that then I suggest you produce it. But first I would like to object to certain members of the jury". Mawgan sounded quite calm.

"You cannot object to the jury. Now just get on with it". The judge ruled.

"I suppose it's better to have a jury of your Hench men than no jury like you normally do when you have young women hanged". Mawgan was still thinking of others before himself.

"Capitan Mawgan it is not in your interest to make comments like that". The judge said quite sternly.

"I don't believe anything I say is in my interest". Mawgan replied.

"Let's get on with it". The judge said to the prosecution.

The man rose to his feet and looked at the Judge. "I would like to call Albert Stoneham my lord". He gave a little bow as he said it.

Albert Stoneham entered the court room and stood in the whiteness box opposite Mawgan. He picked up the bible and swore the oath.

The prosecutor looked at Albert and asked. "Would you please tell the court what the prisoner here told you of the matter in hand"? He then sat down and waited for the answer.

"I will Sir". Albert replied and after a little pause as if to compose himself he began. "I spoke to Captain Mawgan on his return to Cornwall and he told me how he outwitted the authorities he used two ships one unlaidend one laiden with ore which he had stolen. The ore and ship where sold in Spain".

"Thank you Mr Stoneham that will be all." The prosecutor said as he stood up. "I have no further questions my Lord". He said as he bowed to the Judge.

"I have." Mawgan quietly said.

"Make it quick." The Judge said as if he was totally uninterested in anything Mawgan had to say.

Mawgan looked Stoneham straight in the eye across the small court room. "Did the Judge or your father try to get me to take ore to Spain? As I don't believe you had the brains to suggest it on your own". Before Mawgan could say any more the Prosecutor jumped up.

"Objection my Lord". He shouted.

"Yes I should think so". The Judge said as he looked at Mawgan. "You will retract those remarks at once."

Mawgan had a little smile on his face as he replied. "I will not Sir".

"Then I will ask the jury to disregard them and the members of the Public and hold you in contempt of court". The judge had a real look of anger on his face.

Tamasine stood up in the gallery and shouted. "Why should he retract them we all know it's true."

"Through that women out." The Judge shouted.

Two men of the court came over and took Tamasine out she was screaming and shouting but in the end they managed it they just through her down the steps outside.

"Now let's just get on with it." The Judge said as he beckoned to the prosecutor to stand up.

The prosecutor stood up and looked at Mawgan. "You had four ships I believe you still have one the Kernow Mist, two have been bought by a Welsh shipper can you tell the court were the forth on is".

Mawgan scratched his chin as if deep in thought. "Why is it missing"? He replied.

The gallery all gave a little chuckle. "Are you refusing to tell the court, remember you are under oath"? The prosecutor took a step closer to Mawgan as he asked the question.

166

"No sir I can honestly say the last time I saw her she was tied up on the quay". Mawgan didn't say what quay.

"Let's move away from the ship, what do you think of our war in the America's"?

"Personally I think it a total waste of money and life, what's the point of it we have people starving here. We have children on ships and down mines, food that has to be taxed so high that ordinary people can't afford it. And all to rob people of their land, in some far away land that most people have never heard of I just don't get the logic". Mawgan would never falter from his beliefs.

"That's treason talk if ever I heard it". The prosecutor said as he turned to the jury, he then again turned to Mawgan and asked another question. "What can you tell us about an Indian fellow who we believe you took from a ship in Mounts Bay? The man was on his way to London to be tried for treason. He was found in your cottage but with the help of your employees he escaped".

"The man you are talking about can't be the man in my cottage as that man was charged with making love to some noble mans daughter, nothing to do with treason". Mawgan smiled at the prosecutor as he said it.

There were cry's of that's right from the gallery.

The Prosecutor looked at the judge. "I have no further questions my Lord". He said as he sat down.

"No I think we are quite clear of the guilt, I suppose I better ask". The judge turned to Mawgan. "Have you anything to say for yourself"? He asked.

"Would it do any good if I did"? Mawgan replied still with a smile on his face.

"Not really". The judge replied.

The judge turned to the Jury and said. "No one has anything else to say so if you would like to retire and consider your verdict. I don't expect it will take long as there can be little doubt of the guilt".

The jury retired. It was only a matter of minutes before they returned. Not one person had left the court not even the judge. When they returned the Judge asked them. "Have you reached a verdict that you all agree".

"We have". Came the reply from one of the men who stood up.

"Well out with it man, guilty or not guilty"? The judge knew what it was going to be.

"Guilty my lord". Came the reply.

There was a large gasp from the gallery but Mawgan showed no emotion.

The judge put a black piece of cloth over his head and then he looked straight at Mawgan with a look of satisfaction on his face. "Captain Mawgan you have been found guilty of treason, the penalty for this is that you will be taken from this place to a place of execution where you will be hung by your neck until you are dead". The judge took the black cloth of his head before he continued. "I think the hanging should take place in Penzance. That will send a clear message to all those that seem to think you some sort of god, it will show that no one is above the laws of our land. The hanging will take place at nine AM a week to day". The judge stood up and left the court with shouts of murderer being hurled at him.

Outside Tamasine was sat on the court steeps with her head in her hands the tears where running down her cheeks. She got knocked off the steps when the people left like a stampede. Winnie bent down to pick her up as she nearly fell over her as she left the court. "I wonder what your bloody James thinks of this lot now". Tamasine said as she got on her feet.

"Please Tamasine I'm as upset as you but please don't bring James in to it". Winnie put a consoling arm around her.

"I know he isn't like these, but they pay his wage's I just think him as part of it". Tamasine was glad of Winnie's support she knew how fond she was of Mawgan.

As they walked away from the court the two coaches that brought the jury pulled up, and there was Albert Stoneham giving each one of them a coin as they boarded the coach. Tamasine broke away from Winnie and ran over and started thumping Albert on the head. "Bastard! Bastard!" She shouted as her arms were going twenty too the dozen.

Albert pushed Tamasine hard and she fell to the ground it was clear to Winnie that he tried to push her under the horses with his feet as the coaches pulled away. She was quick to get down and pull her clear.

The both sat there on the ground as the coaches and Albert disappeared.

"Come on let's get back and tell the sad news". Winnie stood up and pulled Tamasine up.

It was nearly a two hour ride to get back to Mawgan's cottage where everyone had gathered even Lilly -Rose had made her way up there Lowenna had helped her up the lane.

"We will all have to think about what we can do to free him". Lowenna said as she put her arm around Willy.

"James who had just arrived said. "I don't think there is anything you can do there is no appeal you'll find the court's decision is final".

"Trust me I'll get him out even if I die doing it". Tamasine said as she glared at James.

Chapter 28

Three days had now passed since the courts verdict and news had come through James that Mawgan was now in goal in Penzance. Tamasine had questioned him how many guards are there, are they there all night, are there any windows looking out.

James had told her that he was in an inner cell with no windows two guards from Plymouth sat down the end of a corridor that led to the cell, and that was the only way in or out.

Tamasine decided to go to Penzance she was shore there must be away to get him out. She mounted her horse early and cantered all the way. After walking round and round the gaol for almost an hour it was clear there was no way of breaking him out. She then noticed Albert Stoneham go in.

He had gone in to see Mawgan to ask about Lord Tremeldon's daughter. "Mawgan". He said "I can get you out of this mess all you have to do is tell me where I can find Lord Tremeldon's daughter".

Mawgan replied quite calmly. "If I knew where she was do you think I would tell you and that evil hypocrite that calls himself a father, I 'd hang a thousand times before I'd put her through what you and her father have in mind".

"Well I have given you the chance I'll just have to find a way to get that wench of yours to tell me". Stoneham had that evil smirk on his face.

"Touch her and I'll kill you". Mawgan shouted now quite angrily.

"O' I don't think that likely do you". Stoneham Laughed as he left the goal.

When he got out side he caught site of Tamasine mounting her horse and riding off. He mounted his and followed her. Just outside Penzance he rode up along side of her and grabbed the rains Tamasine's horse reared up and through her off. Stoneham dismounted and leaned over her he grabbed her by the face. "You're going to tell me where I can find Damaris". He said as he squeezed her face hard.

Tamasine pushed his hand off her face. "Go to hell". She said as she started to get up.

She was nearly on her feet when Stoneham hit her hard with the back of his hand drawing blood from her lips. "I think you will tell me". He said quite calmly.

"I don't know where she is". Tamasine wiped her hand across her face wiping the blood from her mouth.

"O' I think you do". He said as he hit her again.

This time Tamasine hit him back as hard as she could.

"It's time I taught you a proper lessen". Stoneham said as he put his hand to his face were Tamasine had hit him. He caught hold of the front of her top and ripped it wide open. He then pushed her to the ground she was wearing a pair of britches, he pinned her arms to the ground with his knees and started to tug at the buttons on the top of her britches. Tamasine was kicking and screaming but Stoneham kept tugging at the buttons every now and then he would stop and hit her hard across the face.

Suddenly there was a shout. "What's going on" It was James.

Stoneham quickly rolled of her. "It's Tamasine I think she has fallen from her horse". He shouted back.

James rushed over and knelt down beside her. "Can you stand up"? He asked.

"I can now that bastard is off me". Tamasine first got to her knees and then stood up she was obviously shaken.

James helped her on her horse but she passed out and fell off, Albert Stoneham had mounted his horse and rode off.

James got Tamasine to her feet she was coming around but it would seem she was concussed he put his arm around her and helped her along the road leading the horse as they went. It took quite some time before they got to Winnie's. "What's happened"? She shouted when she saw them approaching.

"It's Tamasine she has fallen from her horse". James replied as they got to the gate with his arm around her.

"Fell off, my ass!!" Tamasine said her face twisting with pain as she spoke.

"How do you mean, what happened". Winnie put her arm around Tamasine to help her in doors.

"It was Albert Stoneham he forced me from my horse he wanted me to tell where Damaris is". Tamasine sat down in an arm chair.

"Did you tell him"? Winnie asked.

"Of course not if James hadn't come along the bastard would have raped me". Tamasine moved to try and get more comfortable.

"Was he James"? Winnie asked.

"I don't know he was kneeling down beside her when I got there". James replied it was said in a way that Tamasine thought he didn't believe her.

"Bloody hell James he was on top of me when you shouted surely you saw that". Tamasine now stood up.

"I can only say what I saw; I don't doubt your word". James replied he put his arm around her. "Now do you want me to help you down to Mawgan's"?

"No that's fine I can manage thanks for coming along when you did and helping me." Tamasine new James meant well.

"I'll come down with you". Winnie kissed James as she past him and went out of the door with Tamasine.

On the way down she asked Tamasine if she had found away to free Mawgan. "Not yet but I will if it's the last thing I do". Tamasine was still determined he would not hang.

"Just remember if I can help in any way I will". Winnie would also do all she could.

"I know that but it's James, he seems to think that these people are good people, he must have known what Albert was doing to me". Tamasine shrugged Winnie's arm off her.

"Please Tamasine, don't be too hard on James, you always see the worst in him, but he only does what he thinks is right for the country, he doesn't like these people. I know if he thought Albert was attacking you he would have said so". Winnie put her arm back around Tamasine.

172

"I know it's just that he thinks different than us". Tamasine said as she opened the gate at Mawgan's cottage.

"We might think different but we are all honest folk". Winnie said with a smile.

Rajah, Annabel and the children were out in the garden they could all see Tamasine was a little distressed. They came over and both put their arms around her. Tamasine told them what had happened. She broke away from Rajah and Annabel and picked Amy up and cuddled her in. "When is Mawgan coming home". Arthur asked as he put his arms around Tamasine.

"Soon dear very soon". Tamasine was still sure she could free him somehow.

Winnie left and went home and after spending an hour with the children Tamasine went to bed as she was quite exhausted.

The next morning Tamasine was quite philosophic she had thought of a plan and was keen to give it a go she called to Willy. "How many people would it take to sail the Kernow Mist". She asked.

"*Bout* thirty at a push Miss Tamasine". He replied with a confused look on his face.

"I don't think we will have that many but we will have to manage somehow". Tamasine started to count on her fingers.

"Were do *E* want to sail there be plenty of people us could soon get a crew". Willy was confused, why just a few he thought.

"I don't know where we are going but we won't be coming back". Tamasine said still counting on her fingers thinking how few people she had. Neither the less they had to sail her somehow.

"That seems a bit strange to me Miss Tamasine". Willy was scratching his head.

"I'm going to get Mawgan out of gaol, and when I get him out we will have to leave here and there will be no coming back". Tamasine put her arm around Willy "We will just have to hope were ever we end up we can make a good home for us all".

"Just tell us what you want us to do Miss Tamasine". Willy was quite excited.

"You will have to get as many supplies on the ship as possible. Then go to Preacher Jacks and tell Sam and Damaris what we are doing they will want to come with us". Tamasine stopped and thought for a moment.

Rajah and Annabel were listening to what she was saying. "I hope we are included in your plans". Annabel interrupted.

"Of course, but am I being fair on the children taken them to I don't know ware". Tamasine replied she had a large frown on her face.

"Of course who knows we might find a world of peace and harmony, and besides we all owe Mawgan even the children, were would they be without him". Rajah put a reassuring arm around Tamasine.

"Well let's get on with it as I see it there is only going to be seven of us, and the children of course we could do with a few more but I'm sure we will manage". Tamasine turned to Willy. "Now Willy you are going to load the stores, if that bloody Albert Stoneham shows his face try not to let him see what you are up to. I need you to sail the ship out beyond the Mount be there at midnight. Then just two of you row a small boat in to Penzance harbour and wait for me and Mawgan if we aren't there by say two AM just go back and sail the ship back". Tamasine was convinced that wouldn't happen.

"How you going to get him out". Annabel asked wondering if she really had worked that out.

"I'd rather not say for the moment". Tamasine replied with the look of embarrassment.

Did this mean she hadn't worked that out yet they all thought. But no one queried her.

"If everyone knows what we are doing and I can leave the children with you I'm going up and see Winnie and then down and see Lilly-Rose I have to make sure someone looks after the place". Tamasine didn't want the place to fall into the wrong hands when they were gone.

Tamasine got to Winnie's and meet her at her garden gate. "I need to ask you to do something for me. Well it's for Mawgan really". Tamasine said.

174

"You know me I'd do anything for Mawgan". Winnie replied with a massive grin on her face.

"I wouldn't want James to know until were gone". Tamasine said quietly.

"Gone gone were". Winnie exclaimed.

"I'm going to get Mawgan out of gaol tonight and we are going to sail of in the Kernow Mist". Tamasine whispered with excitement.

"Who's going with you and how you going to get Mawgan out of gaol". Winnie thought Tamasine was talking mission imposable on both counts.

Tamasine named who was going and then said. "I'm going to free him with my body. And I have come to ask you, if you will look after Mawgan's cottage and things. I don't see us ever being able to come back, but just encase someone needs to look after his interests".

"My dear Tamasine you few will never sail that ship and how do you think your body will free Mawgan you have never known what to do with it". Winnie was shaking her head as she said it.

"We will sail the ship one way or another, and as for my body I can use it to my advantage when I have too". Tamasine was determined her plan was going to work.

"Well I wish you all the luck in the world I think you will need it, but I'm glad you are trying and if I can help in any other way I will". Winnie put her arm around Tamasine and gave her a hug of approval.

Tamasine left and went down to see Lily-Rose and told her of her plan. "Have you something that will put a man to sleep pretty fast". She asked her.

Lily- Rose left the room and returned with a small earthenware jar. "This will do the trick, you only need a few drops, I have used it on many a sailor when I have amputated there injured legs". Lily-Rose handed Tamasine the jar her wrinkled face smiled.

Tamasine returned to Mawgan's cottage with her precious jar of sleeping potion. She went down in the seller and brought up a small flagon of rum. She removed the top and tipped some away and then tipped her sleeping potion in with the rum and shook it up. "That should do the trick". She said to herself.

Winnie had gone down to the quay to find Willy. He was there with Rajah and Sam loading stores on to the ship. "Is it wise you two out here in the open you could be seen by the wrong people"? Winnie asked full of concern as she stepped on the gang plank.

"O' we are being careful". Sam gave a reassuring smile

"I hope so, now what time are you sailing"? Winnie asked.

"I don't know if I should tell *E* that, *us* don't want that there James fellow finding out". Willy said rather sarcastically.

"You know me better than that no way James will no, I need to know because I'm coming with you. You need as many hands as you can get to sail that ship". Winnie was quite angry at Willy's suggestion that she might tell James.

"Course I know *E* better Miss Winnie, *us* will sail on the seven O' clock high tide, the tides *a'nt* high so *us* only have half hour to get off the quay". Willy new that Winnie wouldn't do anything that would put Mawgan's rescue in jeopardy.

Winnie left and made her way back to her cottage James was just coming out of the door when she got there. "I was looking for you". He said as Winnie came in the gate.

"You found me now". Winnie smiled.

"I have to go to Falmouth so I will be late home tonight". James said as he walked down the path to meet her.

"James I have something to tell you, I don't want you to ask me ware I'm going or who with. I just want you to trust me and remember that I love you and always will. The thing is". Winnie paused then with a frown on her face she continued. "I might not be here when you get back to-night". Winnie said as she put her arms around James.

He leaned forward and kissed her. "That's fine I will see you in the morning". He smiled.

"No James if I'm not here to-night I won't be back ever". Winnie had a tear in her eye as she said it.

"O god, I don't know what to say my life won't be the same without you". James too had a tear in his eye.

176

"Nor mine but it is something I have to do". Winnie held James so tight.

"I won't ask any questions, I know it must be important to you". James was understanding, he knew in the back of his mind it must be a plan to rescue Mawgan, and with all his and Mawgan's differences he didn't want him to hang.

"Come inside we can spend our last hours together". Winnie caught hold of James's hand and led him to the door.

"I think my trip to Falmouth will have to wait until tomorrow". James said rather excited.

Back at Mawgan's cottage Tamasine was altering one of her low cut dresses making it even lower in the neck line. She had the flagon of rum with the sleeping potion in it beside her she would keep looking at it as if she was afraid it would disappear.

Annabel came in to the cottage looking rather exhausted she had been down on the quay helping load the ship.

Tamasine picked up the flagon when she heard the door open not knowing who was coming in. "O thank god it's you". She said clutching the flagon.

"I'm sorry I really startled you didn't I". Annabel looked puzzled to why Tamasine was clutching a flagon of rum. "Surely your plan doesn't include getting drunk". She said.

"O; this" Tamasine held the flagon out in front of her. "Not me but it's part of my plan". She smiled.

"I hope it works". Annabel replied.

"This is the main part of my plan". Tamasine picked up the dress she was altering.

"How is that going to free Mawgan"? Annabel had such a confused look on her face.

"I will just try it on and tell me what you think". Tamasine took the dress and slipped out of the room she soon returned wearing the dress. "Well what do you think"?

Annabel gasped. "You can't wear that".

"O I can". Tamasine replied.

"I can see all your breasts". Annabel looked embarrassed. "When you lean forward I can see all of them, I mean all of them!!" She exclaimed.

"That's good it should do the trick then." Tamasine replied as she wriggled out of the dress and put her other one back on.

"I just hope you know what you are doing". Annabel looked really concerned.

Tamasine smiled at her "Trust me I know what I'm doing". Tamasine paused. "By the way we're is Mala"? She asked.

"She has gone up to see Preacher Jack" Annabel replied.

"She spends a lot of time up there, is he given her lessons"?

"Annabel laughed. "I think Mala is given him lessons".

"You mean her and Preacher Jack are". Tamasine looked surprised.

"Yes I mean her and Preacher Jack, doesn't bear thinking about does it". Annabel laughed.

"I don't think I want to think about it". Tamasine replied.

178

Chapter 29

It was now around five PM. Willy was down on the quay waiting for his motley crew to arrive. Lowenna was by his side, she had made her mind up she was coming with them. The next man down was Preacher Jack. "*Youm* come to say a prayer for us Preacher"? Willy asked as he checked the gang plank on to the ship.

"I'll say a prayer for you Willy lad, but as I see it you need more than a prayer, so I'm coming with you". Preacher Jack replied as he put his hand out for Willy to help him on the ship.

"Glad to have *E* aboard Vicar. I'll tell the crew us in to swear". Willy was quite excited and full of authority.

Next down was Winnie Trewin. "How many crew you got Capitan Will". She joked.

"Well us got three at the moment if *youm* coming. But the *tothers* will be here". Willy replied.

"I'm a coming". Winnie replied she seemed quite excited.

It wasn't long before Rajah, Annabel, and Mala arrived with little Arthur and Amy, they were soon joined by Sam and Damaris.

Willy had a count up. "That's nine of us *tis* going to be *ard* work for us to sail *er* but I know us can do it." Willy was organising his troops.

"Ten Willy!!" Arthur shouted. "I can help sail".

"Of course *ow* did I leave *E* out". Willy ruffled Arthur's hair as he said it.

"Right then Captain Will what do you want us to do"? Sam asked.

"Us need to raze the small sail and untie her from the quay and slowly sail out to the Mount". Willy was scratching his head as if not really sure what to do.

"Come on man just shout the orders and well get her on the way". Preacher jack said trying to give Willy some confidence.

"Right Rajah and Sam climb and drop the front sail. Annabel and Damaris untie us from the capstans. Winnie and Vicar climb and drop the back sail. Arthur you pull that rope in. Lowenna you take the wheel and me and Mala will help with the sails". Willy had now taken proper control.

"I!!I!! Captain". Came the shout after every order.

It seemed to take several minutes but slowly the ship glided away from the quay. Lily-Rose was on the quay side with her clay pipe in the corner of her mouth and waving them off.

"If I didn't know better I would say Lilly-Rose had a tear in her eye". Winnie said as she and the others waved back.

Back up at Mawgan's cottage Tamasine was outside mounting her horse for the ride to Penzance. She had her low cut dress on covered by a cloak which she wrapped right around the front of her hiding any modesty that might be on show. The flagon of rum and potion she had tightly tied to the saddle. She slowly trotted up the lane before galloping of to Penzance.

On arriving at Penzance she made her way to the livery. "Look after my horse". She said to a man who smelled worse than any horse.

"How long for Miss"? The man replied as he caught hold of the rains.

"As long as you want ". Tamasine was undoing the flagon from the saddle.

"How do E mean Miss"? The man asked as he scratched his head.

"What I said I have no more need of him so if you look after him you can have him". Tamasine was saying as she walked out of the livery carrying her flagon.

She made her way over to the gaol which was set back from the quay as she walked along the front she could make out the lanterns on what she thought to be the Kernow Mist. Although very nervous this made her give a little smile to herself. At least that's gone right she thought, she did have concerns about Willy's capability.

Tamasine arrived at the gaol there were two big arched wooden oak doors, she banged hard on them shouting as if she was drunk.

"Clear off". Came a shout from inside.

"I want to see the prisoner". Tamasine shouted back still banging hard on the door.

This went on for several minutes before there was the sound of large bolts being undone. Tamasine quickly undone her cape and through it around the corner she stood nervous in the centre of the doorway with her low cut dress and flagon of rum.

The door opened and there standing in the opening was a rough looking man hair down to his shoulders that looked unwashed and a beard of about seven days. He was about six feet tall and about eighteen stone. "What do you want". He shouted.

Tamasine was petrified but couldn't let it show. "I want to give your prisoner something that will make him smile before he meets his maker". She said in a drunken voice.

"Well you can't know clear off". The man pushed her away from the door.

But before he could shut the door Tamasine was right up in front of him "Please sir just let me give a dying man a little pleasure". She said her voice sounding even more like she was drunk.

Suddenly another voice shouted "Who is it"?

"Some tart wanting to give our prisoner a bit of pleasure". The man at the door shouted back.

"What she like". The voice shouted back.

The man at the door looked Tamasine up and down finding it hard to take his eyes of her breasts. "Like the mermaid you always dreamed of". He shouted back.

"Then bring her in let us have a little pleasure we don't want to waste it on someone that's about to hang." The voice from inside shouted with a tone of excitement.

The man at the door caught Tamasine hold on the arm and led her inside not shutting the door he led her up a dark corridor at the end there was a small table with a man sitting at it. The place was dark just lit by a lantern in the middle of the table. There were two beakers and a stone jar also on the table.

"So you want to pleasure our prisoner *do e Miss.*" The man sitting at the table said.

"O I do Mr" Tamasine replied in a drunken voice.

The man at the table pushed the chair beside him out with his foot. "Best you sit your ass down there a minute". He said pointing to the chair.

Tamasine nervously sat down still clutching her flagon.

"What does *E* have in there"? The other man asked as he tried to take the flagon from her.

"Just a little drinke". Tamasine replied as she put the flagon to her lips pretending to drink. But with her lips tightly closed the liquid ran down her chin and on to her breasts.

The man sitting at the table reached over and put his finger on her low neck line pushing it even lower. "*Caw dam* it Abe you was right *er* sure is pretty as any mermaid". He said as he exposed most of her breast. He then ran his finger up across them were the rum had run down, and then he licked his finger.

Tamasine was now getting very nervous. "Can I go to the prisoner now"? She asked.

The man at the table just laughed. While the other man who she now knew was called Abe said. "Us *avent* finished with *E* yet".

He leaned forward and tried to kiss Tamasine his breath smelt like rotten seaweed almost making Tamasine urge. "Not so fast I think we should have a little drink first". She said as she turned her head away from him and again put the flagon to her tightly closed lips. She then stood up and put the flagon on the table placing her hands also on the table she leaned forward exposing the whole of her breasts. The man sitting at the table picked up the flagon and took three mighty gulps from it and placed back on the table his face looking full of excitement. The other man Abe then picked up the flagon and also had three large gulps and banged it down on the table.

The man at the table took a coin from his waistcoat pocket. "I'll toss *E* to see who goes first". He said.

182

Tamasine started to tremble she thought the potion would have worked right away what if they hadn't drunk enough what if it didn't work quickly she thought. "I think I should decide who goes first". She smiled at the man who was sitting at the chair who had now got up and stood behind her and had but his hand down and was fondling her breasts.

Tamasine was now in a position that she didn't know what to do. She picked the flagon up. "Another drink and then I'll decide who can have me first". She said trying to gain a little time.

The man turned her around put his hand on her chin and squeezed it hard. *Don-e* mess with us *Miss-e"*. He said with a look of anger on his face.

"I'm sure I don't know what you mean sir". She said as she rubbed her hand across his face in a provocative way.

Suddenly there was a thud the man called Abe had fallen to the floor. "Abe, Abe," The man shouted as he went and knelt down beside him.

"Do you think the excitement too much for him". Tamasine said as she forced his mouth open to poor some more from the flagon down him.

The other man took the flagon from her. "*Don-e* waist it on *E tis* only me and you now". The man put the flagon to his lips and gulped another three large gulps then licking his lips. He put the flagon down. "Now miss-*e*". He said as he started to undo his belt. Then suddenly he started to lean forward then he to collapsed to the floor.

A big sigh of relive cam over Tamasine she grabbed the lantern from the table and made her way down a dark corridor she suddenly screamed as a rat ran over her foot. "Mawgan!!Mawgan!! ". She kept shouting in a very low voice that was not much more than a whisper.

She had walked what seemed to her to be ages but finally she came to a cell door. She held the lantern up high and could just make out a figure lying on a bed of straw. "Mawgan is that you". She shouted this time much louder.

"Tamasine". Came a rather startled reply.

"Yes I've come to get you out."

"Where are the guards"? Mawgan asked.

"Don't worry about them they will sleep to morning". Tamasine gave a little chuckle quite proud of what she had done.

"Have you got the key"? Mawgan asked.

"O!! No I never thought I haven't seen one". Tamasine now with all her planning she had forgot the main item.

"The guard with the black teeth keeps it on a string inside his trousers". Mawgan was now getting quite excited.

"They both got black teeth" Tamasine replied.

"The one called Abe if you know which one that is".

"Yes I know the one". Tamasine rushed back up the dark passage. She knelt down beside Abe and tugged at a piece of cord that was tied around his waist with the end going inside his trousers. Out of his trousers came a large key.

Tamasine quickly untied it. As she stood up excited she had the key in her hand a voice said "I'll take that".

Tamasine turned looking rather startled there standing with a pistol in his hand pointed right at her was Albert Stoneham. "You will not". She said as she put her hand behind her back with the key in it.

Albert reached forward to grab her arm; Tamasine stood back and swung her leg kicking Albert hard between the legs. Albert doubled over dropping his pistol to the ground. Tamasine picked it up and ran back down the dark passageway towards Mawgan's cell. Just as she got there Albert caught up with her he grabbed her from behind and pushed her hard up against the cell bars. "Don't mess with me bitch". He screamed.

Tamasine was now had her face being pushed hard in to the bars. Mawgan tried to reach them through the bars but couldn't. "Leave her alone". Mawgan shouted.

"I'll leave her when I've taught her a lesson". Albert said as he pushed Tamasine harder in to the bars.

Albert took his pistol from her and put it in to the belt of his trousers. He then turned Tamasine around he had one hand pulling her head backwards by her hair the other on her chin. He removed the hand from her hair as he pushed her backwards in to the bars, his other hand went down to try and force the key out of her hand. Tamasine tried to throw the key in to Mawgan's cell but it hit the bar and bounced back. Albert didn't pick it up he brought his hand up and hit Tamasine hard across the face with such force her head moved almost forty five degrees with the other side of her face hitting the bars of the cell. As her face came back she spat in Albert's face.

Mawgan put his hand through the bars to try and reach the key. Albert saw his hand come through and stamped on his hand then kicked the key away, still with both hands firmly on Tamasine.

Albert put both hands around Tamasine's throat and lifted her in the air pushing her hard against the bars with his body. "Mawgan tell me where Damaris is and I might let her go". Albert was having pleasure out of this.

Then a soft voice said "Put her down". Then the sound of a pistol hammer being pulled back rang out louder than the voice.

Albert turned letting Tamasine drop to the ground. In the dark he couldn't see who it was. Tamasine kicked the key under the bar to Mawgan then scrambled over to the lantern that was on the floor she picked it up and held it in the air. They were all startled when they saw James Wilmot Sparrow standing there banishing a pistol. "James what are you doing"? Albert asked being surprised at the situation.

"Me!! I'm doing what is right". James replied with a note of contentment.

"You're on our side, the side of the law. Now give me the pistol." Albert held one hand out for James to give him the pistol the other went down to his belt to pull his pistol, he then realised it was his pistol James was holding.

"The law!! Yes I'm on the side of our Kings law. But you and your father along with Lord Tremeldon and his entire crony's aren't the law as I know it. I don't like the smuggling and would try to stamp it out, but what you and your kind do is worse than smuggling. It's just pure personal greed and you'll stop at nothing". James carried on giving a speech.

Whilst this was going on Mawgan had undone his cell door and let himself out and helped Tamasine up from the floor who was gasping for breath. He then put his hand on James's shoulder. "Never thought I would be glad to see you". He said.

185

"Winnie didn't tell me what was happing, but I guessed when I saw Willy loading supplies on the ship. The thought of not seeing Winnie again made me do a lot of soul searching. Leaving smuggling out of it people here are good people, people our country should be proud of. I saw Albert heading for Penzance, and I'm sure if our King knew what was happening he would expect me to do what I have done. My only regret is that I didn't make it known what was happening before. I was too tied up in the smuggling to realise what was really going on". James made meanings to Albert to go in the cell as he said it.

Mawgan pulled the door shut and turned the key. "I hope one day we can show what is happening down here but as for the smuggling". Mawgan was stopped by James.

"Let's not mention that word" he said with a smile.

Mawgan smiled back. He then put his arm around Tamasine. "Come on then let's get out of here". He said.

They made their way out of the goal Tamasine picked up her cloak as they ran down to the beach they could see a lantern being waved to and fro. As the approached they could see Winnie Lowenna and Rajah waiting anxiously for them. Rajah was standing on the beach Winnie and Lowenna where sitting in the rowing boat oars in hand waiting to row them out to the ship.

When they saw them approach Winnie jumped up and jumped out of the boat and ran to James. "James"!! She shouted full of excitement.

"You didn't think I would just let you sail of in to the sunset did you". He said as he put his arms around her and gave her a hug like no other.

Chapter 30

They all climbed on to the rowing boat and rowed hard out to the ship as they approached the ship they could here Willy shout pull that anchor in, raise the main sail. With a reply of I!!I!! Captain, Willy had truly become a captain in a very short space of time.

As they got on board the ship Mawgan was so surprised to see who was there and how they were going about their work. Preacher Jack and Mala were pulling hard on the main sale rope. The sail started to raise, a job that usually took six men. Raja was turning a handle that was pulling in the anchor and young Arthur was over by Preacher Jack and Mala shouting. "Pull" then a pause then "Pull" this went on in rhythm until the sail was fully erect.

Lowenna was at the wheel with Willy standing beside her looking ten feet tall shouting out the orders. Mawgan looked up at him and shouted. "Where we heading captain".

Were ever the wind do take us *cap'n* were ever the wind do take us. Willy replied.

"God I'm so proud of you all". Mawgan had tears in his eye.

"You *goena* to take over *cap'n*" Willy shouted down.

"No Sir" Mawgan shouted back. "Your captain on this voyage".

With Willy shouting orders and every one going about their duties like a well oiled crew they were soon miles out to sea. Mawgan went to the back of the ship his beloved Cornwall was now out of sight. Tamasine came over and put her hand in his. "What you thinking"? She asked.

"Just that I'll be back, it might take a while but trust me I'll be back". Mawgan then turned and looked deep into Tamasine's eyes and then repeated it. "I will return one day"

The ship was now almost to a standstill as the wind had dropped to a light breeze. "I think us should lower the main sale and get some rest". Willy shouted.

Mawgan looked at Tamasine. "Is this really are Willy up there"? He could not believe how well he was doing. "If I still had my ships I would let him sale one". Mawgan said with a smile.

"If you still had your ships we wouldn't be in this situation. All this has come about by your love for others. I keep thinking what if Louie hadn't sailed in that day, and what if those children never turned up". Tamasine gave a big sigh as she said it.

"The world is full of what's and if's, I'm glad Louie sailed in to port if he didn't then Rajah would have hung. And as for the children god knows what would have happened to them if they didn't turn up at your place. They would probably been down the mines or even dead ".Mawgan had no regrets.

"Captain Mawgan I do bloody love you" Tamasine squeezed Mawgan's hand tightly.

Willy shouted down from the upper deck "Come on now all of *E* get some rest me and Lowenna us will take the first watch for two hours". Then Willy looked at Sam. "Will you and Damaris be all right for the second"? He asked.

"I, I!! Captain came the reply.

"Right now the rest of *E* get to your cabins and get some rest". Willy said in a much lower tone.

Mawgan had the captain's cabin to himself, and as there was so little crew they all had a choice of where to sleep. Tamasine shared a cabin with the children. They were both still very excited with their journey in to the unknown. It was quite a while before Tamasine could get them to sleep. When at last they had gone Tamasine got undressed and put a large red over coat on. She sat on the end of Amy's bunk for a while making sure she was fast asleep. Then she slowly crept out of the cabin and in to Mawgan's cabin. Mawgan was lying on his back looking up towards the ceiling as though deep in thought he didn't even notice Tamasine come in. Mawgan was naked but covered with a blanket up to his midriff, his large muscle chest exposed in the dim candlelight. As Tamasine approached his bunk Mawgan looked startled as he suddenly noticed her. "God you startled me you standing there with your coat on". He said looking Tamasine up and down.

Tamasine put her finger to her lips. "Shh" she whispered as she undone her coat and let it drop to the ground. She stood there naked.

Mawgan could not take his eyes of her, her body looked bronze in the dim candle light. You're the most beautiful thing I have ever seen. He said as he pulled the blanket back so that Tamasine could get in.

Tamasine got in beside him Mawgan gently pulled her in to his body until they could feel each other's heart beat. Tamasine whispered in Mawgan's ear. "Well captain Mawgan you've waited a long time but now I think it's time you raised the main sail.

Mawgan now had the one thing he loved more than Cornwall, his precious Tamasine. He all so had the people he loved around him. Where ever they ended up Mawgan knew the future looked fine.